I0717825

The Magic of Yuletide

Edited by Stephanie Osborn and Jon Nials

Chromosphere Press

The Magic of Yuletide

Strawberries in the Snow, Jordan Campbell © 2025

Ice Blue and the Christmas Rescue, A. Kristina Casasent ©2025

A Fairy Christmas, Tiffanie Gray writing as Eppie Gray © 2025

A Fae-ry Merry Christmas, Lydia Sherrer © 2025

A Time for Rest, Aaron Canton ©2025

North Florida is Not the North Pole, Fran Van Cleave © 2025

Christmas on Mars, Richard Cartwright © 2025

Dad's Cookie Jar, Sophie G. Michaels © 2025

Santa Paws is Real?, Sarah Arnette © 2025

The Eggnog Incident, Stephanie Osborn © 2025

Tattered Angel, Dale Kesterson © 2025

ISBN 978-1-950633-41-8 (print)

ISBN 978-1-950633-42-5 (ebook)

Cover art © 2025 Tiffanie Gray

Fiction

First electronic edition 2025

All rights reserved. No part of this publication may be reproduced, stored in a retrieval system, or transmitted, in any form or by any means without the prior written permission of the publisher, nor be circulated in any form of binding or cover other than that in which it is published without a similar condition being imposed on the subsequent publisher. All trademarks are property of their respective owners.

This is a work of fiction. All concepts, characters and events portrayed in this book are used fictitiously and any resemblance to real people or events is purely coincidental.

Chromosphere Press
P.O. Box 252
56 Hughes Road
Madison, AL 35758
www.chromospherepress.com

Contents

Preface

This book you hold was an excited, spur of the moment idea.

I have always loved the Christmas season, and often celebrated Chanukah and the winter solstice as well, in my own fashion. (I do have a chanukiah of my own, incidentally, and have used it—properly—at Chanukah. And with a background as an astronomer, AND having experienced Seasonal Affective Disorder, the winter solstice celebrations are something I can get down with! Yay, sun!)

And when my late husband—who was a professional magician—was courting me, I clearly remember sitting on the floor under my parents' tree with him on our first Christmas together, just talking, and he reached out and plucked a piece of tinsel off the tree—an icicle—and used it to perform a teeny-tiny "cut and restored rope" trick, just for me. I was enchanted.

So for me, this time of year is and has always been very magical, full of big miracles and small gifts of magic.

The book in your hands started out as a series of editing jobs for a friend, who was submitting to a couple of holiday anthologies and wanted me to help her polish her stories first. They were both good, but one got accepted and the other didn't, for reasons unknown. Then I thought, well, why doesn't Chromosphere Press contract it and do something with it? I certainly loved the story; it shouldn't be hard to do something. I offered, she accepted, and then we started talking about what to do with it.

An anthology was the obvious choice, though publishing as a standalone ebook was also considered. But initially we were going to hold it, collect several of her short stories, and publish a sole-author anthology.

That was when another friend suggested opening it for submissions.

I got excited. (After losing my husband, I rarely get really excited about much anymore. Those who are widowed will know.)

So I did.

Even then, I wasn't sure. Chromosphere Press has never done an anthology before, though I have a few planned for the future; it's never been our main product and I don't plan for it to be; we'll always be largely a novel house, while occasionally also putting out my popular science books, which have a following. But despite not having made a reputation in anthologies as yet, we got plenty of submissions, enough to justify putting out a volume of stories THIS YEAR, and here we are.

Normally I'd have opened the call for submissions in the summer for something like this, and thereby make sure we all had plenty of time to do our respective tasks. But the idea came very late in the calendar year—late October—and so it's been a bit rushed. Still, I'm proud of our authors and my staff, especially fellow anthology editor Jon Nials, because everybody really came through with their best work!

I'd also like to say a very VERY heartfelt thank you to my sweetheart of a friend, David Weber, who cheered me on and even agreed to write the foreword! (Thanks to his wife Sharon as well, for not fussing about my taking up a bit of his time!) He insisted on reading all the stories before he wrote it, so he could write an informed foreword, and I was happy to give him a sneak peek, as it were. He didn't even get edited stories! Well, David, here's the complete, polished version, and I'll be happy to personally place a copy in your hands for your and Sharon's enjoyment.

And to the rest of our readers, a Merry Christmas, Happy Chanukah, God Jul, and Happy New Year! May your new year contain as much magic as these stories!

~Stephanie Osborn
Editor in Chief
Chromosphere Press
Thanksgiving week 2025

Foreword

By David Weber

Christmas is a magical time. And this anthology is a Christmas gift that celebrates that magic. Whether it's a misfit elf hunting for Santa's rhubarb pie with a baby reindeer and a troll, or a German Shepherd telling his rescued pitbull baby sister about the mystery of Santa Paws, the things that make Christmas a joy to be shared and a magic to be believed in are spread out toys from Santa's sack.

There is something in this anthology for just about anyone. I'm torn between which one is my favorite, but that's okay. It's Christmas, so like Mabel the young pitbull, who can have as many best days ever as she wants, you can have more than one.

The Christmas Eve when Murphy visited the north pole, which is why Christmas Eve is alcohol free from henceforth by Mrs. Claus's direct decree, has to be very high on anyone's list. And then there's the Christmas on Mars, and the magic of a long family tradition that transfers itself between planets. Or the eleven-year-old Christmas miracle baby who returns to the same gift shop and the same toymaker who created her tattered angel doll to have it refurbished for her injured mom's hospitalized Christmas. The Christmas in Florida when never-met neighbors become friends, the Christmas in Carnifel, when a Maine Coon and a Saint Bernard climb a monster-infested mountain to help a human rescue find his Newfoundland brother. The magic cookie jar for the family who's been associated with Santa Claus for generations. The half-golem daughter of Rabbi Brooks, whose passion is to help others and to prepare for Chanukah.

And at the heart of all of them is love, and cheer, and the joy of giving. Which, after all, is what the Christmas magic is all about.

So dig in. I think you'll find it's quite a feast.

Merry Christmas!

~David Weber

Strawberries in the Snow

By Jordan Campbell

My name is Hilary, of the Hilaris Clan of the Northern Elves. My family has served Santa Claus for forty generations. Occasionally, some of my cousins have worked for Kris Kringle or Father Christmas. So far as I know, none of my family has ever served Sinterklaas or St. Nicholas, except on Sundays, where my brother Hilly plays the chapel's organ. Nobody in my family has ever worked for Krampus, though to be honest, I am not sure whether Krampus actually exists or if he's just a nickname the Boogie Man uses whenever he tries to deliver toys.

I'm not sure where the idea that *only* Santa Claus delivers toys comes from. He's always had help from the others in doing his job. But what a job it is! Delivering toys from a sleigh, riding through the night, thousands upon thousands of miles. It takes a very special person to deliver the toys, and my father says it's our special job to craft the toys that will be delivered.

Or at least it's *supposed* to be my job. There are many, many clans of elves living in the North Pole's villages and every clan has a specific task, a duty in service to Santa Claus and the other Gift-Givers. The Hyreindri Clan tends to and keeps the reindeer herds. The Zingiber Clan grows ginger, which is used for baking gingerbread. The Hilaris Clan, my clan, my family, has one of the most important, most honorable tasks: Toy-crafting.

Or at least it would be an honor if I were any good at toy-crafting. No matter what I do, nothing seems to go quite right. My yo-yos come out as squares; my jack-in-the-boxes try to box their way out; my flying discs go flop. Not one toy I've built is fit even for misfits and I have been at this for decades.

I think I'd be able to work better if I didn't have to do my job with my twin brother Hilton. He is older than me by twelve minutes and is one of the finest toy-crafters in our clan. His yo-yos are so good, the twine never snaps or tangles; his jack-in-the-boxes play a different chime every time a child turns the handle; his flying discs change color as they soar and they always return to the children who throw them. I've even seen him make toys for reindeer, though I don't understand how he does it.

So it was today. Hilton and I stood over a table, carving spinning tops. We'd been working on this for three hours and Hilton was once again proving not only his skill in toy-crafting, but his skill in being a braggart.

"And there!" Hilton laughed in triumph. "That makes three hundred fifty-eight tops for me! How many have you made, Hil?"

I bit my lip as I tinkered with the tops I was carving. I'd only managed to craft about forty. I couldn't help being nervous. Not many children play with tops anymore, but Santa Claus still insists on making and delivering old-fashioned toys. I tried not to glare at Hilton. Santa Claus doesn't like it when anyone argues, and he especially doesn't like it when families argue. None of us like disappointing him in any way. We want to impress him and make him proud.

"This isn't a race," I muttered. "How good can a rush job like that be?"

Hilton's grin grew wider, almost smug, and he picked up one of his tops at random. He set it up so that the point end was on the table. He pinched the top's... top between his fingers and with a twist and a swirl, the top spun. It didn't just spin though. It traveled along the floor, up one wall and kept going until it dangled from the ceiling. My mouth fell open in shock. The laws of physics tended not to mean very much in Santa's workshop, but this was ridiculous.

Everyone else looked up from what they were doing as Hilton spun more tops and sent them along to every corner of the workshop. The tops spun by our cousins, Hilga, Hilo and Halo, who were making dolls and stuffed animals; by our oldest brothers, Hip and Hop, and the electric train they were building; by our youngest sisters, Holly and Hazel, and the plastic baby toys they were crafting.

Everyone oohed and ahhed and clapped. Hilton stood up as tall as he could—which wasn't very tall, we are elves after all—and took a bow. I wanted to knock his hat off his head and tug his pointed ears, but I knew Santa Claus wouldn't be happy if I did that.

"You know, you don't have to show off," I muttered as my fingers fumbled with my top. "I'm...I'm..."

I wanted to say that I was just as good at toy-crafting as Hilton was, but I couldn't. As we Elves are part of the Faerie Folk, we are incapable of lying. I can't lie to anyone, even myself, and that meant that I had to face the fact that my brother was far better at toy-crafting than I would ever be.

I glared at Hilton and picked up one of my tops. I set it up on its point, the way Hilton had done to his own. My top didn't topple over, but when I tried to make it spin, the top wouldn't budge.

"Maybe we can use it for a paperweight," Hilton suggested, the shade of a laugh in his voice. "Or a really big pushpin...there must be some way for it to be useful."

"It's not funny!" I snapped. "I worked really hard on this set of tops!"

I was angrier than I could ever remember being, both at Hilton and at myself. Toys weren't meant to be *useful*. They were meant to bring joy to children. Anything else was secondary. Everyone in my family, everyone in the North Pole, understood this concept.

"You're just... special, Hil." Hilton gave me a smile that was far more condescending than it was sympathetic. I wanted to hit him in the teeth. "Besides, I'm glad it's like this. You being so bad at toy-crafting serves as an example for everyone else for how to *not* make toys. Really, it's rather helpful in its own way."

I didn't hit Hilton, and I'm proud of myself for that at least. But I did stand up so quickly that I knocked over my chair and the table and all the tops we'd carved hit the floor. While mine lay there like a pile of firewood, Hilton's tops began to spin and swirl, each of them a different color or pattern.

"What?" Hilton asked. "It's not like I said something that wasn't true."

"I hope you bite your tongue the next time you eat a gingerbread cookie!" I snapped and I ran out of the workshop, a half-carved top and carving knife still clutched in my hands.

I stomped through the snow, but my footprints didn't leave much of an imprint. I jumped up and down and said as many bad words as I could think of.

"Bad! Awful! Sucky! Stinky!" I screamed. "Terrible! Horrible! No good! Very bad!"

Unfortunately, none of this actually made me feel better. I ran to the nearest snowbank and kicked it as hard as I could. That didn't make me feel better either and all I got out of it was stubbing all my toes at once, through my pointy shoe. I screamed all the bad words I knew again and it still didn't improve my mood.

I stomped past the snowbank and pouted, crossing my arms and frowning as deeply as I could. After I got tired of pouting, I sulked. I got bored of sulking and tried to whine. There wasn't anybody for me to whine to, so I decided to mope instead. After a while, it seemed dopey to keep on moping. I checked my watch. Only twenty-six minutes had gone by since I had left the workshop. Well, that was that, I supposed. Elves aren't able to lie and most of us need to keep busy, or we'll go crazy.

I suppose I could go back to the kitchens and get a snack. Strawberry rhubarb pie was my very favorite food, but I didn't think they were making that today. I sniffed the air, since I wasn't that far from the kitchens. I could smell gingerbread, of course, and eggnog and peppermint bark and peppermint ice cream and peppermint candies. But no strawberry rhubarb... I shook my head. I really did need to go back to work.

But as much as I wanted to get back to work, I was too embarrassed to face everyone in the workshop. I didn't *need* to work with Hilton—and truth be told, I often tried to avoid working with him specifically, because he was such a showoff—but I wasn't just nervous. I was afraid and worried that I'd mess up whatever other toy project my family members were working on.

Maybe there was something else I could do, maybe even with Santa Claus. He was always needing help in his office, checking his Naughty List and his Nice List. Some of the other Gift-Givers might even be visiting. Christmas Eve was only two days away, and Santa Claus would need to discuss his travel routes with the others.

Santa Claus lived in the largest house in the village surrounding the workshop. It could be difficult to tell where the village begins and the workshop ends, but I knew the whole village like the back of my own hand. Everyone worked together and almost everyone lived close together too. It was sort of like those company towns that had existed a long time ago, in faraway places. I don't know very much about them though, beyond that the owners of the company towns were all so naughty that Santa Claus didn't even give them coal. He wrote them letters saying he was disappointed in them instead. I'm not sure how well that ended up working, since most people don't believe we really exist.

I walked along and as I did, a great gust of wind blew in my face and I coughed and hacked and turned my face so I could spit. I hated cold gusts of wind and the worst part of it was, I couldn't tell whether it was a regular gust of wind or if Jack Frost was acting up again. I took another step but the wind grew stronger and stronger and the next thing I knew, I was in the air. I didn't even get a chance to scream as I was tossed about.

As I was flung through the air, I couldn't help but think of the toys I'd crafted that were meant for flying. None of my kites had managed to stay in the air for more than a minute or two—and somehow, some poor little boy named Charles always got them, and they invariably got eaten by a tree.

At last I landed, right outside a set of large windows. Jack Frost had already done a number on the windowpanes, and I wondered whether I might be able to help Santa Claus by washing his windows... and for that matter, his windowsill. It was covered in cookie crumbs and candy cane bits. I started to get up, but then I heard voices and I crouched back down. I don't know why I did it, since I wasn't trespassing, but I hid all the same.

"So, it's settled then? I'll take the Eastern Seaboard and you'll handle the Midwest and stop in the Rocky Mountains?"

"As far as North America is concerned, yes."

"Thank you, Kringle."

Santa Claus *and* Kris Kringle? I could hardly believe my ears and I clung to the windowsill. It wasn't really eavesdropping, even if it was private. Santa Claus and Kringle always got together to plan their routes.

"I'll take care of Western Europe and the old territories."

That voice was deeper and sounded richer. It could only be Father Christmas! My goodness! My greatness! My super-duper-ness! Three of them, together? It made sense, of course, but it was still amazing.

I knew a bit about the other Gift-Givers. Kris Kringle lived to the west and he rode a stallion and fought monsters with a sword when he wasn't delivering presents. Father Christmas lived even further north and always wore green instead of red. He also sent plenty of rich foods for a feast after Santa Claus finished his deliveries. Sinterklass and St. Nicholas lived even further away, in even odder villages: Sinterklass's people lived in treehouses surrounding a river and St. Nicholas's village all lived in one ginormous tower.

"Is that all settled then? Santa Claus, are you well?"
The wind picked up and I strained to hear the conversation. Santa Claus sounded older than usual and a lot more tired. I wanted to help him.
"Every year, it seems... my age is catching up to me... my knees hurt more often than they don't."
"You can take another mantle, Santa... it would rejuvenate you..."
"You know why I can't do that, Kris... what I need is something for ruh..."
The wind howled so fiercely that I had to cover my ears and I couldn't hear the last bit, but it was enough. Ruh... ruh... something. It must be rhubarb. I scurried from the window as fast as I could, which wasn't easy with all the snow. I was so excited that I hardly noticed.

This was it! My chance to show them all! I would show all my brothers and sisters and all my cousins and every other member of my family that I could do things just as well as Hilton could. Even if it wasn't toy-crafting, I'd show them all and then Hilton would have to eat a big slice of humble pie. And I'd be able to help Santa Claus, that was the most important thing.

Rhubarb, that had to be it. I couldn't think of any other words that started with a "ruh—" sound. That wasn't so hard, so long as I followed the instructions. The Hilaris Clan rarely baked, since that was the Zingiber Clan's responsibility. I grimaced as I remembered an incident a few months before. One of the Zingiber elves, Zorri, tried to create a new flavor of cookie because she was tired of oatmeal raisin. She used sundried tomatoes and porridge instead and the cookies hadn't tasted good at all...but they had made excellent hockey pucks.

I didn't want to make the same kind of mistakes that Zorri had—it had taken a month for the smell of sundried tomatoes to get out of the kitchen. I didn't want to get in the Zingiber Clan's way either—this was their busiest time of year and they were baking all sorts of goodies for Santa Claus and the others to deliver. I decided that I'd have to gather the ingredients and do the baking myself.

Rhubarb pie... so tart and so sweet at the same time and when the pastry was just right, nice and flaky on top, but with a firm crust... it was the tastiest food in the world. I bet it almost tasted as good as the food they ate up in Heaven!

I started walking towards the reindeer stables. I figured I'd speak to someone in the Hyreindri Clan about where I might gather the rhubarb... and strawberries too. You couldn't have rhubarb without having strawberries. I stopped stomping entirely. The reindeer were much bigger than us elves and I didn't want to be stepped on or kicked in the face or run over or eaten if any of the reindeer got spooked.

I walked and walked and walked and then I walked some more until I finally came to the stables. Dozens and dozens of reindeer lived here, and not just the ones that Santa Claus used to lead his sleigh. There were never just eight or ten reindeer and I have no idea where humans got that idea in their heads either.

"Hilaris Clan, eh?" one of the Hyreindri elves asked. It wasn't a surprise that he recognized me. All members of the Hilaris Clan wear red, while all members of the Hyreindri Clan wear bright blue. "Delivering more toys from that Hilton fellow?"

"No, sir," I said, hoping beyond hope to steer the conversation away from my brother. I wouldn't be able to lie if the Hyreindri elf asked me any questions. But maybe I could ask him questions instead. "Your name, sir?"

"Flippy," the elf replied. "And you're just in time to help me feed the reindeer. Grab the other end of that trough."

The trough was very heavy and it took me a long time to help Flippy move it. When we finally did get it into position, Flippy took to filling it with hay from a nearby haystack. I grimaced as a bit of hay flew into my mouth and I spat it out. I never understood why the Hyreindri Clan used hay as a food for reindeer. It didn't taste good. After he finished loading the trough with hay, Flippy began layering the trough with vegetables—carrots, parsnips, turnips, yams. Pretty much anything you'd expect to be at a Christmas dinner.

"Is there any rhubarb?"

"Why would there be?" Flippy asked. "That's been out of season since July."

"Strawberries then?" I couldn't help but ask. Flippy looked at me like I had two heads. "Um... never mind... that's out of season too, isn't it?"

"Since June!" Flippy declared. "Now, let's get back to work."

Strictly speaking I didn't *have* to do that. It wasn't my family's job to tend reindeer. But I was an elf and that meant working hard, so I did as Flippy said. Together, with a few more elves from his clan, we loaded almost twenty troughs of food. We had just finished when someone blew a horn, and the reindeer began filing in.

There were all sorts of reindeer... tall ones and short ones, ones with antlers and ones without. They were all sorts of colors—tawny brown and tan and chocolate and cream and a few were even black. There was one at the end, smaller than any of the other calves, that was white. I thought at first that the calf was just covered in snow, but then I realized he was shaking too badly for any snow to stay on him. Several of the Hyreindri elves escorted the herd into the stables and a couple of them were limping.

"It was an accident," the little white reindeer squeaked. "I'm really sorry!"

"Nobody ever said it was intentional," one of the Hyreindri elves replied. "But that doesn't change what happened, Bou."

"Just give me another chance, Flossy!"

Flossy? Flippy? Do all of you have names that start with F? I was hardly in a position to judge, given my own family always picked names that started with *H*. I shook my head and turned back to the little reindeer calf.

"That's not something that can be done," Flossy said sternly. "This is not a punishment, Bou. It's more that we simply think you're better suited elsewhere."

Elves couldn't lie, but there was no way that I knew of that would make those words actually sound nice. Bou's ears drooped and he began to cry and stomp his little hooves in distress.

"I'm being reassigned to Antarctica!" Bou wailed. "I'm never going to get a chance to fly!"

"You're not being reassigned to Antarctica," Flossy retorted and I saw him rub at his temples. "Just eat your food and then have a nice nap, okay?"

Flossy didn't say that very nicely and that made me wonder about just how nice a nap he could possibly expect Bou to have. I held my breath until Flossy and Flippy and the other elves were on the other side of the stable and I crouched down low.

"Spinach, why do I always have to eat spinach? Okay, so I like it best and nobody else will eat it and it'd be bad to let it go to waste..." Bou muttered and mumbled as I got closer. "It's not fair, not fair at all. No matter what I do and no matter what I try, I always make a big mess."

I glanced over my shoulder to make sure that I wouldn't be overheard, but none of the other elves paid us any mind.

"Hi," I said, as Bou sniffed at a very large piece of kale.

"I've already been lectured to by four different elves," Bou squeaked. He made a face, but I wasn't sure if it was at me or at the kale. "I really don't want to hear any more. Go away."

"I don't want to scold you," I replied. "I want to help you."

The words were out of my mouth before I had even realized what I was saying... but I meant them. Elves cannot lie. It's one of the reasons Santa Claus likes us helping him. It was why my brother's words were so awful—they were true. The words that the Hyreindri elves had told Bou were true. I needed to prove myself and so did this little reindeer.

"How can you?" Bou asked. "It's not like you can make me fly."

That was a very good question. I watched as Bou ate the spinach, kale, and hay. I tried not to grimace. Elves stuck to a diet that tended to have lots and lots and lots of sugar. My cousin Half-Gallon Hank could chug two quarts of hot chocolate in a single sitting. I had a weakness for spicy cherry candies myself. A few of my cousins were oddballs and only ate fruits and vegetables and I wished they were here with me now. One of them could probably get through to Bou more easily than I could. I couldn't lie, but that wasn't the same thing as always having the right words.

"Besides," Bou shook his head. "Santa Claus only has eight reindeer to pull his sleigh. He doesn't need any more than that."

"That's not always true," I told the little reindeer. "Santa Claus swaps out the reindeer he uses all the time. Sometimes the Gift-Givers don't even use reindeer. Santa Claus has to use kangaroos when he visits Australia."

That was something I still didn't entirely understand, though apparently Father Christmas wasn't welcome in Australia at all and Kringle refused to go there on principle. There was a smaller village with its own workshop somewhere in New Zealand, but I'd never visited. The elves that lived there were a bit bigger than the ones in the North Pole and we'd heard rumors that some of them liked to go on adventures and climb mountains and volcanoes.

"If you're trying to make me feel better, it isn't working." Bou shook his little head and a bit of spinach dangled from his lip. "Elves can't lie and the other elves told me that I'd never be able to be big enough to fly and guide Santa's sleigh."

Not big enough... not good enough...

I knew how that felt, or at least, close to it. No matter what I tried, it always seemed that Hilton was always going to be better than me and all I did was mess up. I was wasting time here. I needed to find some rhubarb somewhere, and some strawberries too, and Flippy had already told me that there weren't any since they weren't in season.

"All I wanted to do was to be helpful and maybe do something special for Santa Claus," Bou whimpered. "He's the most awesomest person ever and he deserves so much more than what he gets."

My heart clenched and I reached out a hand to pat Bou on the head and scratch him behind the ears. Maybe I could help Bou by making him help me so we could both help Santa Claus...

"Bou," I whispered, my mouth forming a grin. "Are you up for a little adventure?"

Most of the elves I knew weren't much for going on adventures. We stick to the village with our toys and our sweets and our reindeer. But not all elves were like us. The elves that lived in the village in New Zealand climbed mountains, and we had other cousins who had even grander adventures than that. The svartalfar elves were taller and stronger and faster than us, and instead of crafting toys, they crafted grand, fantastic weapons and fought all sorts of monsters. My clan? We mostly try to run and hide when there's danger and we rarely go looking for trouble.

I led Bou away from the stables and back to my family's house in the village. I had read enough stories about adventures to know that it never hurts to be prepared, so I decided to gather as many things as I could think of. I took rope, a flashlight, a trowel, a book of matches and some wax, some needles and thread and a thimble, yarn, and two canteens full of hot chocolate.

"Can you think of anything else?"

"A towel?" Bou suggested. "We could use a towel."

I wasn't sure what good a towel would do, but I got one as Bou suggested. I pulled on an extra coat and an extra scarf as well, and then fitted a woolen hat over Bou's head. It fit well enough, since his antlers weren't due to grow in for over a year.

There was the matter of food and I handed Bou a Christmas orange, which he ate in a single bite. I gathered food that was good either hot or cold, so that meant oranges and roasted chestnuts and plenty of fruitcake.

"I think we have enough," I said. "I'm ready if you're ready."

"What about bear spray?" Bou asked. "There's grizzly bears and polar bears and they can eat us up in a single bite."

"Bears are in hibernation this time of year," I answered. "I don't think we'll have to worry about that."

It wasn't that I disagreed with Bou that bears could be dangerous—except for teddy bears, which I wasn't very good at crafting—but I could only carry so many supplies at once. I gathered everything up into a very large Christmas stocking and strapped it to my back. It had been the middle of the day when I'd first run out of the workshop, but now it was nearly sunset. As far north as we were, I would have thought it'd be nighttime pretty much the whole day long. But then again, the laws of weather tended to matter as much as the laws of physics in Santa's village.

Fresh snow had fallen and twinkled like ten thousand tiny diamonds against the beam of light from my flashlight. Jack Frost had apparently settled down and the winds had calmed. Bou bounced ahead of me, almost like a little goat instead of a reindeer.

"An adventure, an adventure, an adventure for..." Bou paused. "Wait, what are we looking for exactly? Strawberries and rhubarb? Neither of them is in season. Shouldn't we get something else for Santa Claus? A new sleigh with rocket booster jets? Or maybe something for his beard? Beads for Santa's beard!"

"No, no," I giggled. "We'll have to... think of something. But Santa Claus needs rhubarb so he can feel better."

The question was *how* to get the rhubarb if it wasn't in season. There were lands beyond Santa's borders, beyond the villages where the other Gift-givers lived, that might be worth trying. I'd heard stories of wonderful forests and valleys where it never got cold, where other faeries lived. Maybe we might even find something magical to use as secret ingredients for the strawberry rhubarb pie—the teardrops from a phoenix or a unicorn.

I took another step forward, and my pointy shoe slid on ice. I didn't have time to even realize what had happened before I fell. I stumbled and twisted, falling head over heels, tumbling and turning. I rolled over and over again and left the trail far behind. I heard Bou crying my name but I couldn't answer him. I saw the sky and then the snow and then the sky again and then the snow again. Finally, I saw nothing at all—I'd slid and tumbled down the icy patches and over a cliff. My scream never left my mouth as I fell. I hit the ground and bounced three times before I finally stopped moving.

Every inch of me ached. I ached in places I didn't even know were places. The world spun around me so much, I felt like one of Hilton's tops. I almost thought I'd rather be in the workshop, watching my brother show me up, than be here with my everything broken.

"Wow! The sky had a baby!"

A voice... a single voice. Much deeper and rougher than any elf I'd ever heard. I tried to get up, but the voice called out.

"No, Sky Baby! Don't get up! You might have boo-boos!"

"I'm not a baby!" I shouted. At least, I tried to shout. It sounded more like a squeak. "And my name is Hilary!"

I figured it had to be a good thing that I was able to argue at all, but when I tried to move my arms and legs, I couldn't make them budge even an inch.

"Hilary... oh, is your daddy a hill?"

"How could my father be a hill? He's a toy-crafter!"

I needed to get out of here, as far away from the voice who belonged to someone who thought I was either the sky's baby or a hill's baby. I needed to find Bou and get back to the mission of finding strawberries and rhubarb. I needed to help Santa Claus. I needed help myself.

"Oh, I can help you! I want to be a helper!"

Something huge grabbed me by my legs and lifted me up and out of the snow as easily as I'd pick up a carving knife. I was set right back on my feet and I was so relieved it took me a minute to realize who had helped me.

"Thank you... you?"

It wasn't a human who had helped me out of the snow. It wasn't an elf or a dryad or a leprechaun or dwarf or gnome. It was something, *someone*, who I had never seen before. Ten feet tall, four times my own height, and covered in thick fur over gray skin, and a pair of curved, yellow horns. It was a troll.

Elves and trolls are about as different as any two groups of faeries can be. Elves are small and trolls are big. Elves eat candy and sweets. Trolls eat raw meat and bones. Elves work for Santa Claus and bring joy to children everywhere. I've never, ever heard of any troll that was kind or helpful before.

"You... you... you..." I stammered, searching for the words. I couldn't lie, but I didn't want to say the wrong thing and make him angry by accident.

"Me!" The troll grinned, revealing rows of sharp teeth. "Nice to meet you! You're one of Santa's elves! I always wanted to meet an elf! I always wanted to meet Santa Claus! Oh, it's nice to meet you! I hope it's nice for you to meet me! My name is Knobby Knuckles Kneecapper the Ninth! But my friends call me Knobby!"

That was... this was all right. I could work with this. Knobby seemed almost excessively friendly, but that wasn't a bad thing. I decided the best thing to do was to introduce myself, but as soon as I said my name, Knobby burst out laughing.

"Oh, I knew that already!" Knobby grinned. "You just told me a minute ago when you were still stuck in the snow! Don't you remember?"

Before I could reply, Bou burst through the trees, nearly toppling over on his little legs. He bleated and turned towards me.

"Oh, Hilary, I was so worried! I thought you'd fallen and gone splat and it would have been all my fault because I couldn't fly down to catch you."

"I did fall, but I didn't go splat," I assured Bou. The little reindeer trembled where he stood and I reached out to pat him on the chin. "Our new friend Knobby helped me out of the snow."

New friend... I wasn't able to lie. I glanced at Knobby, who gave me a wide, toothy grin.

"You saved her? Oh, thank you! Thank you..." Bou jumped back so quickly, I almost thought he might have flown. "An ogre!"

"An ogre? Where? I've never met an ogre before either!" Knobby looked around and scratched his head. "Oh, me? No, I'm not an ogre. I have a penpal who's an ogre, but he lives in a swamp a long, long ways away from here, and I've never left this forest."

I glanced around—there were trees everywhere. Fir trees and pine trees and larch trees and trees I didn't know the names of. I wondered just how far we were from home.

"Thank you, Mr. Knobby," I said. "Bou and I had better be on our way. We need to find rhubarb and strawberries to make a dessert for Santa Claus."

"I'll come with you!" Knobby declared. "I always said I wanted to meet Santa Claus! And this way I can get him a gift!"

I glanced at Bou and we exchanged a quick nod. There was no way that Knobby was going to leave us alone now that he knew what we were doing, so we may as well let him come with us. Besides, we could use the company.

Knobby liked to talk. Knobby liked to sing. Knobby liked to talk and sing and tell stories that he made up on the spot. He didn't like goats very much, since he didn't like head-butting things. I concentrated on staying on the trail. It wasn't easy keeping up with Knobby, since it took three of my steps to match one of his.

"Strawberries and rhubarb," I repeated. We'd only been out for a couple of hours but it felt like it had been twelve days. "There has to be some place where we can find them..."

Unfortunately, I hadn't thought to bring a compass or a map. I couldn't be sure where we were, exactly, and whether we were any closer to any other forests that would be more temperate. My fingers fumbled as I reached for my stocking. Somehow, nothing had spilled when I'd fallen off the trail. I took a drink from my canteen and then handed it to Knobby. He took a fistful of snow and poured a bit of hot chocolate on it and then shoved the melty snow into his mouth.

"Not bad..."

He handed the canteen back to me, so I could give Bou a drink, but Bou stared straight ahead, not moving. At first I thought he'd gotten too cold to even move but then I realized he was staring at something. And not just any sort of something. He was staring at a bear.

The bear was *huge* and had fur as white as Bou's. A polar bear then... the biggest, hungriest predator in the whole North Pole. The bear looked up at us and opened its mouth, wide enough to swallow me whole. The polar bear roared at us, but then Knobby stepped in front of me and Bou, spreading his arms.

"ROAR!"

The polar bear reared up onto its back legs. It was taller than Knobby was and roared again, louder than any bear I'd ever heard. Knobby seemed impressed and excited, while Bou stood there frozen with fear.

"Wow! Good one!" Knobby inhaled sharply. "But I can roar even louder than that!"

He spread his arms out even wider and bellowed, so long and so loud, I was astonished that he didn't have to stop to take a breath. Knobby was making his challenge to the bear, defying it to come any closer. I turned my head and shut my eyes. I didn't want to watch what would happen next. Knobby had more courage than I could have imagined, but I didn't want to see him get hurt. But then, both the bear and the troll stopped roaring at each other, and I heard another voice.

"What's all this fuss about?"

I opened my eyes and watched as a tall man walked up to us, almost casually. He was very tall, but also rather thin. He had a thick beard, almost as thick as Santa Claus's. The polar bear bowed its massive head and nuzzled the man gently. My jaw dropped and Knobby rubbed at his eyes.

"I trust my companion Ursus was not too unpleasant?" The man chuckled. "He can be a bit temperamental at times. You three look quite chilled. Come and join me and my brothers for our feast."

I'm not sure what made me trust the stranger so, though if I were being honest, I wasn't sure that he was a stranger. He led us down the trail toward a clearing where a large bonfire had been set up. The bonfire was among the most beautiful I'd ever seen. Eleven other men were gathered around it, each accompanied by an animal. I saw an Arctic hare, an Arctic fox, a fully-grown reindeer, a pair of lemmings, a snowy owl, a sea eagle, a white wolf, a musk ox, a puffin, a fur seal of all things, and an enormous brown bear.

Some of the men were young, only a bit older than me, and several others were older, with short beards. Some wore thick coats, but others were dressed in thin, warm clothes.

"Brothers, we have guests," the old man who had led us to the bonfire declared. "May we make them feel welcome?"

"As welcome as they make us," a young man said cheerily. He petted the lemming on his shoulder. "Always picking up strays, are you, November?"

"March, you say that as if you wouldn't do the same," another man said. He had brown hair and grew his beard in a goatee. He raised a mug of apple cider. "Now then, to friendship!"

"November? March?" Bou asked. "I don't understand."

"I do," I replied. "These are the Twelve Months... they're the twelve sons of Father Time. They're kin to Jack Frost."

"Really?" Knobby asked eagerly. "Oh, how wonderful! I always wanted to meet Father Time! And the Twelve Months too!"

"Aye!" Another Month declared. "And what brings you three out here? We don't normally get visitors."

"Please sir," I replied. "Bou, Knobby and I were trying to find a more temperate part of the forest, where we might find strawberries and rhubarb to make a pie for Santa Claus."

"You make an odd set of companions," one of the older Months said. His beard was streaked with silver and he scratched his wolf behind the ears. "An elf traveling with a reindeer is one thing, but a troll?"

"They're my friends," I said and I was struck by my own words. I couldn't lie. I glanced at Knobby. He had stepped in front of a polar bear for me... he was far braver than I was. "Please don't talk about Knobby that way. Thank you for your hospitality, but if you continue to cast judgment against Knobby, we'll be on our way."

My pointed ears burned and I felt Knobby place a hand on my shoulder. He was so much bigger than me that his hand pretty much covered my entire arm.

"Ah, courage!" One of the youngest Months said. "I love it when they talk back to the grown-ups while still being polite."

"Aye, friendship is a precious thing," the older Month agreed. "You speak well, April. Now, for this task of yours. You will not find the strawberries and rhubarb you seek without help."

I bit the inside of my cheek and looked from one Month to another. The musk ox lumbered toward me and I held as still as possible.

"May? June?" December said. "I think an hour of your time should be sufficient. Let us help these three out a bit."

Two of the Months stepped forward. They were older than me, but not so old as to have full beards yet. They nodded at one another and held out their hands. Behind me, a patch of snow about twelve feet square melted away at once and two strawberry bushes sprouted up in less time than it took me to have spoken to the Months to begin with. A minute later, a thick bush of rhubarb sprouted as well.

Bou, Knobby and I set to work at once, plucking as many strawberries as we could. They were small as berries went, only about the size of the tops I'd tried to carve, but they were heavy, dense with juice and flavor. One of the Months kindly handed us a bucket and we filled it very quickly. After the bucket was full, we pulled up stalks of rhubarb from the ground and Knobby tore off the leaves. The strawberries were as red as rubies and the rhubarb a dark pink that reminded me of peppermints.

"Now all we need to do is get back to my family's house to actually make the pie," I said. "Christmas Eve is in two days... or one day. Is it past midnight yet?"

That didn't matter that much. We had our supplies and our plan. I could finally, finally do something really right for Santa Claus.

"I don't know how I could ever thank you," I said, turning to the Months. Tears pricked at my eyes. "But you've helped me more than you realize."

Bou, Knobby and I set off again, our supplies in hand. It might have been my imagination, but it didn't seem nearly as cold as we walked our way back to the trail. I could have sworn that the breeze that picked up was summer warmth, rather than the nippiness of Jack Frost.

I trembled as I held the pie. The scent of strawberries and rhubarb, mixed with spices, was enough to make my mouth water. Knobby was too big to fit easily inside my family's house, but he stood outside our kitchen and sniffed it through the open window.

"That smells absolutely amazing," Knobby said. "And when will we give it to Santa Claus?"

"Very soon," I said. "Christmas Eve is starting on Earth in less than an hour."

I returned the pie to the counter and got out a thermal-lined tin to put it in. The pie was piping hot, but I didn't want...

"Hilary?"

I grimaced. Hilton stood in the doorway. I sighed. I had known this was coming, but that didn't mean I had to like it.

"Where on Earth have you been? You haven't been in the workshop. You haven't been crafting toys. You're bad at that, I know, but—"

"All over the forest, that's where I've been." I answered honestly, cutting him off. "I was on a mission to find strawberries and rhubarb and I made new friends. There's a troll named Knobby who is one of the friendliest people I've ever met.

"A troll?" Hilton asked, his eyebrows rising towards the crown of his head. "I have never heard of a friendly troll, Hilary."

It wasn't a lie, necessarily, especially since up until just two days before, I had never heard of a friendly troll either, but it still made me grind my teeth.

"I don't need your permission to make friends," I said. "Hilton, please, this pie is going to get cold."

"Hilary, that is not a good idea!"

I ignored him and pushed past him. I met Bou at the door and Knobby joined us as we walked down the path. I heard Hilton cry out in alarm and I wondered how he could have missed Knobby, who didn't try to conceal his appearance.

We ran down the street until we came to a tremendous crowd of elves. Santa Claus would be setting off in his sleigh soon. I elbowed my way through the crowd, apologizing a bunch of times. Bou bumped and kicked and butted his way through. Knobby was big and strong enough to just pick elves up and set them down gently to clear a path for himself.

I was going too fast to stop now and I tripped over my own feet at the edge of the crowd.

Santa Claus, Kris Kringle, Father Christmas and St. Nicholas all stood side by side, looking down at me. Four of the greatest Gift-Givers of all time.

"Santa Claus!" I gasped, bowing to him. Santa Claus was practically the King of the North Pole and you had to bow to kings. That was the rule. "I bring you a gift..."

I held the pie up and I felt Santa Claus gently take it from my hands. Slowly, he undid part of the lid and sniffed at the pie.

"Strawberry rhubarb?"

"For you, sir," I answered "I wish to give to you, since you give so much to others."

"Excellent!" Kris Kringle said and Father Christmas nodded sagely. "This smells delicious!"

"With due respect, sirs," I said. "I intended this to be for Santa Claus specifically. I know that rhubarb is something that he enjoys very much."

"Rhubarb? Ho ho ho," Santa Claus chuckled. "So you're the little elf who was eavesdropping by my window. And it was you that borrowed one of my reindeer?"

"He said I was one of his reindeer!" Bou squealed, jumping up over my head—which wasn't very high, all things considered. "Oh boy, oh boy!"

"Yes sir..." I admitted. "I did not intend to invade your privacy at first sir, but I..."

I didn't finish my sentence, since I wasn't able to lie. My mouth went clammy and my ears burned. I had eavesdropped, but it had wound up being for the best, hadn't it?

"I am sorry, sir."

"And I forgive you. As it happens, you misheard me," Santa Claus said quietly. "What I was talking about was my rheumatism was getting more severe."

Rheumatism? Not rhubarb? I'd gotten it wrong. I'd gotten it way wrong. All that I'd been through and I had let Santa Claus down.

"I'm sorry sir," Hilton called. My ears burned hotter than ever. I hadn't even heard my brother approaching. "I hope that you will not judge my family for the actions of my sister. She has always been different from us... she's special, I believe, and doesn't always act the way an elf should."

"That will do," Santa Claus said coolly and the other Gift-Givers turned stern as well. "I happen to think that Hilary is very good at being an elf."

"She's awful at crafting toys, though," Hilton said. "And she broke rules, sir. I love my sister, but that does not mean that she is easy to get along with, or that she does not cause a lot of trouble."

"She reached out in kindness to me and to others," Santa Claus said. "It has been a long time since I have been given a gift from anyone other than Mrs. Claus."

"And it's something you didn't actually ask for," Hilton continued. "So how good of a gift is it, really, sir?"

"I've heard enough arguments from you," Santa Claus said. "Hilton, you're going on my Naughty List. If you talk back to me one more time and say something mean about your sister, I'll have you stand in the corner."

For the first time that I could remember, and I could remember back a great ways, my brother was speechless. Bou continued to bounce this way and that, from one Gift-Giver to the next. Kringle reached out a hand and rubbed the top of Bou's head.

"What happens now?" I asked, and as I did, I heard the other elves begin to murmur amongst themselves. I felt Knobby shift around next to me.

"A troll, an elf and a reindeer calf..." Father Christmas murmured. "That is a bit of a conundrum..."

"They can come with us," Kringle suggested. "Goodness knows you could use the assistance, Santa Claus."

"I think that's an excellent idea."

My ears burned so hot that they might have actually been on fire. I couldn't believe what I was hearing. Fly with Santa Claus? That was an honor that I never dared to even fathom. I trembled as I watched Santa Claus scratch his beard thoughtfully.

"You do?"

"I can't lie any more than you can," Santa Claus said. "I think that you are quite a fine little elf, Hilary."

"Indeed," St. Nicholas agreed. "For what is Christmas but the holiday of holy reconciliation. Your kindness and friendship shine as an inspiration for all."

The Gift-Givers nodded at one another. I wanted to stand but I wasn't sure if I remembered how to do that. Bou bounced up and over my head and then Knobby pulled me back up. He looked nothing short of ecstatic.

"Come along now, we've got a long way to go," Santa Claus said, clapping his hands. "To the sleighs!"

I looked all around. The clans had all gathered to see Santa Claus and the other Gift-Givers off. Now they all stared at me, and I couldn't help but think that they might think it was crazy. Hilton stared at me, his expression unreadable. But then they all started to applaud.

Four sleighs, drawn with a dozen reindeer each, were ready to be driven out into the night. Sinterklass would not be joining us this time, but I could hardly contain my excitement as I followed Santa Claus along. He patted several of his reindeer, greeting them by name, before he got into the sleigh. Bou bounced.

"I don't think there's room," I said. "Knobby, you can go and... oh!"

"Hilary, you are my friend. My best friend. I will not take from you in any way and you are going to live your biggest dream to help Santa Claus," Knobby said as he lifted me up and set me down next to Bou. The little reindeer hopped into my lap while Knobby looked inside the sleigh. "Are there seatbelts?"

"Never mind the seatbelts," I said. "Santa's magic sleigh's never needed them. What about you, Knobby? It isn't fair to you to miss out on this."

"He can come with me," Kris Kringle called as he fitted a pair of goggles over his head. One of the lenses was blacked out and it almost made him look like he had an eyepatch.

"Oh, what fun! We'll see each other soon, Hilary! Bou, be happy and bouncy!" Knobby wrapped his arms around me and Bou and squeezed us so tight, I wondered if we might burst.

"I may be a bit when we reach North America," Kringle said. "I have a spare bit of business to attend to in Chicago."

"Oh," Knobby cried out in joy. "I always wanted to go to Chicago! They have pizza in Chicago!"

Apparently, Kringle had a taste for pizza as well and he and Knobby started debating crust styles and toppings. Santa Claus chuckled and with a flick of his wrists, the reindeer guiding the sleigh began to trot. Soon, they started to gallop and in no time at all, we were flying. Bou nuzzled my cheek and he bounced... and he didn't come back down to my lap, but hovered in midair.

"Hilary, I'm flying!"

I burst out laughing and wrapped my arms around Bou. He was flying... Knobby had gotten to meet Santa Claus and go to Chicago... and I was helping Santa Claus more directly than any elf from the Hilaris Clan ever had. I laughed harder than I had ever laughed before... glad tidings of joy bubbled in my belly.

Far below, I could see the elves of the North Pole gathered, my clan among them.

"Merry Christmas!" I called, waving to Hilton, to my other siblings, and all my cousins. "And to all a good night!"

Ice Blue and the Christmas Rescue

By A. Kristina Casasent

My tail wrapped around my legs, I was thinking about closing early on Christmas Eve when the little, bedraggled Rescue crept into my office.

At the time, I wasn't sure how old the Rescue was. Standing, we would be eye to eye. But sitting in the office chair, he had to look up at me. Bending his head back like a baby bird, his mouth was half open. But he was quiet—for the moment.

He shook red strands from his green eyes. Green eyes in a Rescue was good. That matched Feline eyes, like mine. A Rescue with the dark eyes of a Canine, almost without white, would look silly. But the round pupils and white that surrounded them gave Rescues a constantly nervous, startled appearance. But what could one expect from those who weren't from Canifel?

The Rescue entered my dim office from the dying brightness outside, bringing with him the scent of trepidation.

His frail Rescue eyes were slow to adjust to the dim interior. He stood staring at nothing for many flicks of my tail. When he finally spotted my smoke-colored, furry body, his eyes widened, showing even more white than normal in a Rescue.

Truly, we Maine Coon Felines are the height of Felinicity.

"Sir? Mr. Ice Blue?" He spoke in the high-pitched voice of the young. His scent—his scent was fear. "I'm Billy. Can you help me, sir?"

My mane fluffed and let my tail twitch in agitation. *I don't do Humans.*

"I don't handle Humans." I kept my voice flat, a mild hiss my only sign of displeasure. "Look elsewhere."

"It's not for me." The boy's face blanched. "It's my big brother—"

"I said, I don't handle Humans."

This time, his face hardened.

"Bear—I mean Charcoal Snack is not a Human. He's a Newfie. Black with a white starburst on his chest." The boy held a hand just above his waist. "He's about this tall—Wait..."

This time the hand was held as high up as the pink hand could reach.

"He's bigger here. But he's still my brother."

I think I decided to help Billy and Charcoal Snack then, since I reached over and raised one of the window blinds. I didn't need the extra light. But Human eyes were weak and needed twice the light to see half as well. The light lit his pink, furless face, and the sharp scent of fear receded a bit, letting me breathe easier. My mouth hadn't gotten the message yet that this Christmas I would bend to help a furless Rescue.

"I don't handle Humans. Especially ones that can't even remember to use your brother's proper Canifelian name."

The Human flushed, and a brief wave of scent told me he was embarrassed.

"He was Bear for years before we got here. We've only been here a few days. We don't even really know anyone yet. And it's Christmas Eve—"

"Humans!" I could smell my own annoyance this time. "You brought Christmas! And Santa! The Canines think it's wonderful—they get stockings full of treats. We Felines, we know the truth. Nobody spies on us and judges us. Knowing what we do, day and night. Nobody. And now!"

I turned in a tight circle on my office chair, my tail lashing.

"Now, our young learn their magic on Christmas Eve! All from Human interference!"

The young one shook his head. His hands, seemingly acting on their own, found the pockets in his denim jacket. His blue jeans rode above his ankles, showing sturdy, if well-used, brown hiking boots.

I glared at him, with just the tip of my tail twitching now. I licked a paw and patted down my puffy mane. There was no reason to explain just how insulting it was to be spied on, to be watched, judged, and marked down on a list. How could one knock an offending cup off a table if one were constantly judged? How could one save their dignity when they missed a jump? Oh, Canines and Humans didn't understand the need for balance—one could not be nice if one was never naughty.

"Spying on you?" He slowly gravitated to the window. "You mean Santa? You're worried about Santa? B—"

My tail twitched, a sneer twisting my whiskers.

"Be—Charcoal Snack went up Snow Mountain." He gulped and looked away.

I followed his gaze out the window—he was staring at the largest land feature in this region of Canifel.

"He was looking for a place for us to move. Someplace quiet. Maybe with people we could make friends with."

"Nobody lives on Snow Mountain except monsters." I spoke more quietly. "It always has snow—so there's no melting to make toboggan runs or anything that might draw Felines or Canines—or even Humans—up there. The lakes are too far and not particularly popular."

I paused, and the Human Rescue—Billy—continued staring out the window as the sunlight slowly faded towards dark.

"How long has he been up there?" I could smell the scent of fear growing.

"I'm not sure." The boy pulled an old, beat-up, brick-like cellphone from his pocket. "I lost battery days ago. But he left early this morning. While it was still dark."

With his last sentence, the bouquet of nervousness in the air increased even more. My nose itched to sneeze. I used a paw to rub it, as if straightening my long whiskers. *Whiskers are useful and attractive.*

The silence lasted long enough for the little Rescue to relax. I broke the quiet.

"I'll help you. But I need something with his scent."

The small Human whirled from the window, his face quickly going from somber to happy, even if his too-white eyes stood out, giving him a scared, pathetic look. The joy gave way to confusion.

"Something with his scent? Are you like a scent hound then?"

My fur bristled, and I felt my ears go back. I felt a rumble build up in my chest. The words spat out, harsh. "I... am not... a hound."

"I'm so confused." The boy took a breath, his scent sharp, like over-ripe citrus.

Poor little Rescue. I curled my tail around me, pulled in each claw with an effort of will, and let the box-like chair do its calming work. My words were soft when I spoke.

"My magic is to locate a person or item by scent."

"So, you're not a scent hound, but you follow his scent?" Hugging his denim jacket to his sides, the Rescue still looked confused.

"I now see your confusion." I laughed, this time at myself.

"You're new to magic, right?" Without waiting for his response, I continued. "My magic allows me to know the location of a being by smelling something of theirs. I don't have to follow a scent. There doesn't even need to be a scent trail. I just need something to smell."

"Charcoal Snack doesn't have any clothes..." The thin, ragged human bit his lip, looking thoughtful, his face all scrunched up.

I blinked slowly, waiting with the patience only Felines can display. My face was impassive, and my tail was trapped under one paw to hide its flicking.

"We don't know anyone here." His face cleared suddenly.

"Bear lets me sleep curled up with him." A warm, cozy scent floated momentarily across the room. "He says it's to keep him warm, but I know he's keeping me warm. He doesn't really like it warm. I don't think any Newfie does."

With superior Feline intelligence, I quickly grasped his point. Gracefully leaping down from my box chair, I stalked up and looked directly into his eyes.

The strange white and green eyes met mine calmly and firmly. He was not full grown yet, but he matched me in size already. *Humans.*

Lowering my head slightly, I delicately sniffed his jacket. *Not to be confused with the inelegant snuffle of a Canine.*

The young Rescue smelled mostly of Human of course. But I could smell Newfie fur and dander. Plus, of course, a lot of drool, which was splattered across the jacket arm and shoulders.

A light but distinct aura formed around the child and me. Clean and white-blue, the outline slowly faded.

In my mind's eye, two locations formed.

One was right in front of me. *Rescue. Human. Billy.*

The other—I felt and saw the location clear in my mind, the cold wet snow below my paws.

My head turned as my eyes sought out Snow Mountain. The young human hungrily followed my gaze.

"He's still up there, isn't he?"

I nodded, Feline fashion.

"In the pass near the peak. Where the monsters nest."

"Monsters?"

"I think some samurai from your world came here long ago. They encountered monsters on our side. The Japanese called them oni. Demons. Monsters." I shook out my mane as I went back to my desk.

The Rescue didn't need to respond. His look and his scent told me everything.

"Big, hulking bipeds. Red skin and big teeth. Short, brutish horns—usually two. Some have more or less." I took my seat and considered him. "Are you afraid?"

"No."

Considering what I could smell, he lied. Before I could respond, he added something that made me think he'd eventually adapt well to Canifel—given that Canines and Felines could both smell how he really felt.

"Well, yes. But that won't stop me."

With that, we headed up Snow Mountain.

Of course, it didn't happen that fast.

First, the Rescue needed proper clothing. Not being a Feline nor a Canine, he lacked the fur to actually survive on the mountain otherwise.

And then I had to introduce him to Chartreuse Apple, my business partner. The Rescue walked up totally unintimidated by the giant Saint Bernard, two feet taller than he was. Even with his brother being the same size, most humans took more time to get used to new giant breed Canines.

Chartreuse Apple, even seated, was still taller than the boy. Her brown and white fur stood out against the dimly lit walls. She already had on her side carry bags. In Canifel, we do not call them saddlebags.

"This is Chartreuse Apple."

The boy walked up and offered his hand, into which Chartreuse Apple placed her paw. And they shook.

Obviously, he'd been learning something about Canifel, since he knew that Canines shook while we more refined Felines did not.

His white-rimmed eyes scanned her up and down.

"You're the same size as my brother. His fur is longer and darker, though. And he drools a lot more."

"Not drooling as much helps with my magic." Chartreuse Apple gave him a Canine nod.

"What's your magic?" The human's white eyes exaggerated his perplexed look. Chartreuse Apple shook her jowls as she stood.

"I can heat liquid, so any sort of tea, coffee, or hot chocolate you'd like, I'm your girl."

"That's really useful. Especially now." The boy laughed and shivered as Chartreuse Apple opened the doors to the outside, letting in the icy evening air.

"Useful now," Chartreuse Apple barked out a laugh, "but not as much during the summer."

We all started moving through the doors, leaving the dim light for the darker outside. I smelled the tension flowing through the air from the boy. He kept glancing at the gray sky, as if expecting it to cave in on him. I brushed by, offering a little comfort. But I left most of the comforting to my people-pleasing business associate.

Soon, we were out past the houses, past the cleared streets, and on to fresh, uncracked snow. Our pace and the glinting of snow in the twilight seemed to distract the boy, since the sharp scent of his nervousness faded.

Chartreuse Apple moved out in front of us to break trail. She was much better built for it—blocky, large, and hardened. One of the few areas for which Canines were built better than my Feline, graceful form. She and I discreetly put the boy between us, since he needed the most help.

As we walked, though, Chartreuse Apple continued to talk to the Rescue. Canines were like that—always ready to talk to someone new.

"How did you get here? To Canifel, I mean."

"Well," the boy giggled, "it all started when we decided to go look at the Marfa lights."

"The Marfa lights?" Chartreuse Apple's ears immediately perked up. "So, you're from Texas?"

"You know about Texas?"

I could smell the surprise even though I couldn't see his face.

"Yes," I broke in. "We all know about Texas here. Texans won't pipe down about Texas. It sounds interesting—I guess—pretty big, pretty hot, and pretty flat — but one can only stand to hear so much about it."

My two companions snorted at me. I don't know why, but I'll get them for that.

The big Canine huffed out a breath—I'm sure she noted my raised fur and flashing eyes.

"Yes. We get Texans here. They're very proud of their country." She pushed forward, and we plowed after her.

"Well, it's technically what we call a state." The Rescue continued his story. "But it's like another country."

He stepped around a particularly large mound of snow. I, more elegantly, followed him with a quick, graceful leap.

"So, we were looking at the Marfa lights," he smiled, "And Charcoal Snack started chasing a firefly. I ran with him. We had a lot of fun chasing it. But he went around a bush, and he disappeared into a hole in the air. Well, it wasn't really in the air. A hole in... It was just a weird hole."

Chartreuse Apple shook her ears.

"We know what you mean." I flicked my tail, even if neither could see. "We are used to seeing rents in the fabric of space all the time. They're difficult if not impossible to describe—even when you're used to them. A hole that isn't a hole is a good enough description."

"But when he ran in," the boy shrugged, "I followed him because I had to take care of him. He's my Bear. I mean, well, Charcoal Snack is my brother, my best friend."

I decided to let the lapse slide this time. My business partner, being a Canine, didn't really care about proper names. Not like we Felines do. I'm pretty sure T.S. Eliot made it to Canifel at least once, and his books had made it back to us.

Eventually, we reached the traditional resting spot. Chartreuse Apple didn't really need to stop.

My claws were matted with wet. My tail was sprinkled with snow. And my whiskers had picked up icicles. But stopping wasn't necessary. And I certainly would never admit to a desire to stop. *Never.* Canines could not be superior to us Felines. The thought was unnatural.

But our tag-along, being only Human, really needed some sort of rest. His teeth were chattering. His breath was coming in short, shallow huffs, but he did not complain. Felines and Canines are both just better at moving quickly than Humans are.

The resting spot was near a cave. As we approached the entrance, I could smell the boy's fear return. He stood outside and looked into the yawning mouth of blackness. His voice was a thin whisper.

"It's really dark in there."

"It's a cave." Chartreuse Apple, being upwind, just grunted. "Caves are dark. And cool."

I started to respond when a thundering, roaring noise interrupted, drowning out my reply.

Oh, garbage day.

I looked up and just got out a shout, "Snow—!"

Then it barreled into us.

Snow. Rocks. Branches. Ice. Everything.

I saw the boy slammed into the rock face outside the cave. Chartreuse Apple and I were hit full on by the falling mountain of snow. We were smashed into the cave. I slashed out with my claws. The roaring swallowed me up. I remember seeing stone whooshing by overhead, as I was carried through the cave entrance.

Into darkness.

I woke up cold.

My fur was plastered against me.

My ears tingled from cold.

My nose could smell nothing but ice and winter.

And the dark—a black so deep that even my Feline vision saw nothing.

I lay there trying to get my bearings and attempting to move, which I couldn't. The snow pressed down in all directions. The air was too thin. Then I heard rumbling. *Monsters!*

Being Feline, of course, I didn't panic.

It's normal to struggle when you're trapped. My claws raked out, trying to cut my way out.

Then something grabbed me.

I could feel every individual fur strand on my body stand up.

But the something resolved itself into the boy's hands. He had a jacket and a hat that we'd given him, but he didn't have gloves. Gloves are rare in Canifel. But he was digging with his pink, furless fingers in the cold snow. I could see he had dug four or five feet down.

"Ice Blue! Are you okay?" When he finally saw me, his worried expression relaxed—even if it was hard to tell with the Human's enormous eyes.

I shook my head and looked up against the glare of the yellow light and started to reply. "Of course, I'm—"

Light? How could there be light in here?

In the middle of this thought, the thin human dragged me out of the snow pit and hugged me. I'd never been hugged by a human before. Or really by anybody or anything in Canifel. My fur went all up again at first, and my claws came out.

But I managed not to use them on the boy—on Billy.

Eventually, it was kind of nice. I'm sure that was just because it was warm, and I'd been so very, very cold.

I gave a little sigh, and a purr rumbled out, unbidden.

Looking over Billy's shoulder, the light was weird. It was a strange yellow glow. It was nondirectional because there weren't any shadows, which made it really—weird. I'm not sure how it appeared to human eyes, but to our superior Feline vision, not having light shadows makes it difficult to see. No contrast. No depth.

I managed to croak out, "Light?"

Billy looked around and then laughed.

"Oh, that's me."

"What?"

I'm a Feline. I should be more eloquent.

"Let's find Chartreuse Apple, and then I'll tell you about it." Billy waved his red, snowy hands around.

"Good thinking, Human." I always give credit where credit is due. Humans and Canines needed the encouragement after all.

We moved about a bit.

It was a little hard to see the tip of Chartreuse Apple's tail sticking out of the snow without a shadow to set it off. But we eventually found said tail and immediately started digging. We worked our way down her tail, around her hips, up to her shoulders, and we got into the neck when she finally noticed us.

Go figure. A Canine buried in snow takes a nap.

We woke her up, and she backed out of the small snow cave that had entombed her. She noticed the light too and started to ask.

"I'll t-t-tell you ab-ab-about it lat-ter. So c-c-cold." Billy stuttered, his teeth chattering.

Chartreuse Apple immediately went into rescue mode and hustled him through the cave back outside.

I followed along.

The Saint Bernard got Billy to lie down and then flopped carefully on top of him. A big dog warms you pretty quickly. It's one reason I work with her. Although I would never tell her that.

While she did that, I climbed up on her back and dug through the side bags she carried. I pulled out a big metal tin filled with liquid. *Can you call it hot chocolate when it's cold?*

I put the tin out near Chartreuse Apple, and she concentrated on it—a soft green glow enveloped the tin—while I went into her bag again. I returned with three cups. One Human and two for Canines and Felines. Ours were much more elegant, wider and shallower than the Human one.

By the time the hot chocolate was ready, Billy had warmed up enough to tell us his story.

"I remember being hit by the snow and slamming into something, and then everything went dark for a while. I woke up, and y'all were gone." He waved at the cave mouth. "I was pretty sure you were somewhere in the cave because that's where all the snow seemed to go."

This time, it wasn't fear I smelled. It was embarrassment and a little bit of shame.

"I... I don't like the dark. It took me forever to get into the cave to start looking for y'all." He took a deep breath. "But I made it. And it got darker and darker. And my mind started to—it—everything closed in on me. But I kept pushing forward because I needed to help y'all."

He shuddered, and Chartreuse Apple flopped closer to him.

"When I thought I couldn't stand it anymore, suddenly, it seemed like I could see a bit better. And bit by bit, that yellow light just got brighter and brighter. It got really bright, and I remember thinking, *tone it down*." Billy waved around the hand that was not holding a cup of hot chocolate.

"And it dimmed. And then it started getting too dim, and I thought that I wanted it brighter again. The light actually started getting even brighter again. That's when I realized I was doing it." He stopped and looked thoughtful.

The non-directional glow came back for a few seconds. Brightened. And then slowly dimmed out.

"After that, it was a matter of going through the caves and looking for you two. I found Ice Blue first. He was buried really deep, but I think he woke up enough to claw at the ceiling as he was being pulled along because I found claw marks too small to be yours, Chartreuse Apple, but they looked proper for a Maine Coon Feline."

After a pause for some more hot chocolate, he continued.

"I dug around until I found Ice Blue and dug him out. Then he spotted you, Chartreuse Apple. You were a lot easier to handle because your tail was still sticking out. One of the benefits of being a horse-sized Saint Bernard, I guess."

We all chuckled at that, each in our own way, more from post-crisis letdown than from it actually being funny.

As Billy concluded his tale, we finished our hot chocolate. Then we turned back to the mountain path. At least now we didn't have to worry so much about snow slides.

Too bad that what we would find was much worse.

As we climbed the mountain, the sunlight continued to flee. The light levels grew dimmer and dimmer. This time, I didn't smell any fear from Billy. Instead, the non-directional yellow light came back.

"That's great, Billy." Chartreuse Apple laughed and shook her head. "That'll let me go even faster."

With that, she started galumphing through the snow. This had the added benefit of keeping Billy warm as he ran after her.

I followed behind, staying out of the worst of the flying wet snow. Then we turned the corner and found it.

A large red monster.

This one stood ten feet tall, bigger even than the biggest Great Dane or Mastiff I'd ever seen.

It had three—no, four—horns sticking out of its head.

Nasty, brutish black hair covered its head and face.

With a roar, it charged us.

The three of us dodged out of its way. Billy went to the right and rolled into a drift of snow, which fell over him. The soft yellow glow disappeared.

Well, he'll get better at that with time.

Chartreuse Apple leaped to the left. She landed on top of a drift and disappeared straight down into it.

And me, I dodged straight ahead, right between the monster's feet.

It whirled uncertainly and roared again.

I was the only one not covered with snow at that point, so it turned to chase me.

As I continued running up the path, I heard the meaningless barking of a Canine coming down the path toward me. This was followed by actual words.

"Don't worry. I've got it." With that, a big black shape with a glowing white star on its chest leaped over me. Charcoal Snack—there couldn't be two Newfies on this mountain—tail held high, ran past me, dodging the monster's curved claws at the end of thick, stubby fingers.

The bounding Newfoundland dog curved around behind the demonic red creature, which whirled to follow him.

The Newfie shook his head, throwing drool everywhere.

In a burst of gray light, Charcoal Snack ran up the snowy drift. Literally, he ran up the side of the drift instead of falling into it like Chartreuse Apple had.

The monster chased after him, only to stomp right into the drift. The oni's red-orange skin disappeared until only its horns poked out.

Billy's brother continued down the other side.

I ran between two drifts—not even Feline elegance could keep me suspended above snow—just in time to see the monster break through the far side of the drift.

It roared and charged.

Charcoal Snack was still working on luring the monster away from the rest of us, for he ran in a circle several times around the creature as it flailed at him.

Then, running by and thwacking the monster with his tail, he ran toward a shiny field of ice beyond. *A frozen lake!*

Great big Newfie paws clawed up the snow amidst a gray glow as he plowed onto the ice, never slipping, never sliding.

The big red monster followed close behind him, reaching out to grab the Newfie.

Just as the claws closed around the end of the Newfie's tail, the monster gave a horrid roar. His front foot sank beneath the once still waters of the lake.

I realized this was a warm volcanic lake, one of the few reasons why people would climb Snow Mountain.

Charcoal Snack shook his head and trotted back calmly atop the water, going around the red monster, who disappeared into the depths. His tail lowered from where it had been during this chase, to hang behind him as was normal for a Newfie.

The water returned to its ice-like stillness behind him.

By the time our Canine benefactor reached shore, Chartreuse Apple and Billy had joined me on the side of the water.

Billy's soft yellow light lit up the reception party.

As Charcoal Snack touched shore, Billy hurled himself upon his brother. They embraced as only two siblings could embrace, even if one was a Canine and one was a Human.

The big Newfie's tail rose again to wave softly back and forth in complete contentment.

Charcoal Snack gave one big lick to Billy.

"I'm sorry. It's so nice and cool here. I fell asleep." His tail and ears sank as he spoke.

I gave Chartreuse Apple a meaningful glare, and her ears and tail drooped too.

"It figures they'd both get their magic on Christmas Eve. Interfering Humans." I glared at Billy this time, even if he didn't notice.

Chartreuse Apple's head tilted and blinked at me more like a cat than a dog. I responded to the unasked question.

"Billy's brother, he can walk on snow or liquid water without falling in."

"Who are these two?" Charcoal Snack turned big, dark Newfie eyes on the two of us.

Billy whirled, smiling.

"This is Ice Blue." He pointed at me.

"That," the Human waved a drool-covered hand at my business partner, "is Chartreuse Apple."

"They're my friends." He hugged his brother again.

I blinked, a little surprised. *Friends?*

I realized that Billy had become my friend.

The Human had grown on me.

Like a Christmas tradition. Or maybe mold.

A Fairy Christmas

By Eppie Gray

"It's just not fair, Merry," Eileen whispered into Merry's soft blue and purple mane.

Eileen held tightly to Merry, her stuffed unicorn. She had been complaining to her mom and dad, then crying to Merry for days ever since she found out they were moving from the house she had grown up in to a place several towns away.

Far from her friends and school. Far from the places she knew and played.

And all of that right before Christmas!

"At least I'm not losing you, Merry. You'll always be there for me."

The moving truck pulled up into the front yard, and Eileen's mother called for her to come into the house. Eileen hopped off the swing, placing Merry on the seat to wait for her, and ran to the house, her feet crunching through the leaves that the wind was blowing from the trees.

Everything had been so busy and happened so fast that it was in the car on the drive to the new house that Eileen realized Merry was missing.

"Mom! Dad! Merry's not in my backpack. We have to turn around! We have to go back!" Eileen sat forward as far as the seat belt would reach so that her parents would hear her.

"We can't go back right now, Eileen, we have to be there when the moving truck arrives at the new place. Besides, I'm sure that Merry just got put in a box or in your suitcase. I'm sure we will find her after we get there," Eileen's mother tried to reassure her.

Eileen sat back in her seat and rustled through the blankets again, seeing if just maybe Merry had gotten rolled up in them, but there was no sign of her favorite unicorn. Tears welled up in her eyes and slowly ran down her face. The thought of losing Merry along with everything else was just too much. She really hoped that her mother was right.

Two days later, Eileen still hadn't found Merry. She had gone through the boxes and her suitcase. She had looked in the kitchen boxes and the living room boxes. She had searched the back seat of the car in case Merry had gotten pushed under a seat. Merry was nowhere to be found. Eileen had cried herself to sleep every night, even though her mother and father tried to comfort her. Her father had even brought her a little white unicorn, but it wasn't the same as Merry at all. Her mother had called the real estate agent for her to look in the house and around it, but they had said that they hadn't found the little stuffed unicorn.

Each call and each answer just made Eileen sadder and sadder. Her mother had found the Christmas decoration boxes and suggested that they put the decorations up. Eileen usually loved helping to decorate, but it wasn't the same this year. Finally, Eileen's mother asked her to put a red ribbon on the front door, as they hadn't had time to make a pine wreath this year.

Eileen took the ribbon from her mother and went outside to hang it on the hook. But the hook was too high for Eileen, and that was just the last straw for the day. She ran over to the wooden fence that separated their yard from the neighbor's yard, and she sat down on the dry, cracking leaves. Eileen dropped her arms and head onto her bent knees and cried.

She felt someone stroke her hair, but not saying anything. It felt nice. She finally looked up, expecting to see her mom or dad, but it was a pretty, red-haired stranger. Eileen was worried for a moment, but the lady with the green eyes smiled at her and then waved at someone. Eileen looked over and saw her mom standing on the stoop, and her mom waved back. So her mom must know the lady.

"Hi, I'm Noelle. I live in the house next door and I heard you crying. I thought you might be hurt, so I came over to check. You are hurt, just not on the outside, right?"

"Yes. I lost my unicorn, Merry. And all my friends at my old school, and everything!" Eileen's voice started rising as she spoke.

"Oh, that is a lot of hurt inside," Noelle said to Eileen. Noelle sat down on the ground facing Eileen. "Sometimes it is very hard to make new friends when you are missing the old ones so much."

Eileen nodded. She wiped a tear with the back of her sleeve.

"Well, it doesn't seem like life can go backwards, so you will need to make new friends. But sometimes it's a little easier if we can have an old friend to talk to while we figure it all out." Noelle smiled at Eileen.

"But how? I have looked everywhere for Merry."

"Well, there are folks who live in the wilds who go everywhere and see everything. And sometimes if you are a kind person they will help." Noelle looked to see if Eileen was listening. Eileen nodded her head cautiously. Noelle went on.

"The fairies are very tiny and hard to see, but they listen. And if a child was to wish upon the first star of the first snowfall, then they are more likely to hear. And while it may not happen right away, if you are kind, then they will try to help with their wish."

Eileen's eyes were enormous as she listened to Noelle's story. Even though she was a grown-up, she seemed very serious about fairies, which was strange to Eileen. But somehow she felt Noelle was telling the truth.

"I think you are freezing out here, Eileen, let me help you with that ribbon and then you can go inside and finish helping your mother." Noelle stood up gracefully and reached out a hand to help Eileen stand.

Eileen thought that Noelle's hands were very warm even though she had been outside with Eileen. They took the ribbon over to the door, and Eileen handed it to Noelle, who then hung it on the hook.

"Don't forget, the first star of the first snowfall." Noelle turned and went down the stairs and around the fence over to her own yard. She waved one last time before she went inside her house.

Eileen thought a lot about what Noelle had said about wishes and fairies and old friends and new friends. Her mother opened the door and shooed her back inside, with a cup of hot chocolate waiting for her.

Eileen got up from her bed and wrapped her blanket around her shoulders and went over to sit in the window of her bedroom. Outside it was dark, far darker than where she had lived before. She looked up, but couldn't see any stars above. She wondered about Noelle and the fairies. She wondered what fairies even looked like?

Something caught her attention, and she realized the moon was shining down between cracks in the clouds. She looked and looked for stars and finally saw one as it twinkled.

Should I? Should I wish?

And then, she saw a single snowflake drift past her window, slow and dancing, sometimes up and sometimes down and sometimes spinning. The star winked once more, and Eileen knew it would be covered by clouds again soon. She closed her eyes and made her wish.

"I wish that my Merry would come back to me!" Eileen whispered. She opened her eyes, and there were sparkles everywhere, dancing in front of her window. Her father must have turned on the outside lights. The star was gone, and the snow was falling harder.

Eileen hoped Noelle was right.

FeatherSnow, one of the leaders of the snowfairies, heard a whispered child's wish upon the wind. She caught the snowflake with the wish in her tiny hands and looked into the shiny crystals. There was a white unicorn with a blue and purple mane and tail and blue eyes, that was very missed by a kind child.

FeatherSnow tossed the snowflake back up into the air and with a bit of fairy magic it went streaking off across the sky like a falling star. She followed after it to see where it led.

It went very far across rivers and fields and forests. The snowflake paused finally over a yard with a gigantic tree and a rope swing with a wooden seat hanging from a big limb. FeatherSnow flew down to see what the snowflake was waiting for.

FeatherSnow found the blanket of leaves with only the horn of the little stuffed unicorn barely peeking out. She quickly moved around, fanning her wings to fluff and rustle the leaves. Little by little, the unicorn was uncovered.

Just in time, as the first snowflake drifted down.

FeatherSnow gently directed the wish snowflake to land on the unicorn lying there, all dusty white body, black hooves, gold and silver horn, blue and purple mane and tail and blue eyes.

Blue eyes sparkled and then blinked as the snowflake touched it and melted into her face, light as a kiss from Eileen.

Merry sat up and looked at the shiny, glowing creature hovering in front of her. She had never seen such a thing, or really thought any thoughts. But along with the magic came the words she needed. The snowfairy smiled sweetly at her.

"Oh good! You are awake! Your girl, Eileen, misses you so much and made a wish that you would return to her, to be together."

"Eileen, she loves me very much," Merry replied. She knew it in her heart. She looked around at the snowfairies that were gathering around her. They were all very beautiful, and that made her heart smile, too.

"Yes, she does, so now you must go find her," FeatherSnow said.

"How do I find her? I don't know where she went."

"Right this way, Merry," several of the snowfairies cried out at once. And they began swirling in and around, dancing with the snowflakes that were falling faster and thicker now.

Merry watched them and stood so that she could dance too. Her feet shuffled strangely, as they had never walked before, much less danced. But she slowly got the hang of it and was soon trotting along, staring up at the tiny snowfairies as she went.

Soon Merry was out of the yard and down the driveway and prancing along the sidewalk. She was in and out of shadows as a car would come by now and again in the darkness. She loved the sparkle of the snowflakes and the snowflake fairies. She loved the feel of the crisp night air blowing against her fur and running through her mane. She loved the cold, wet snowflakes as they pressed against her horn and settled on her lashes.

Merry gave a whinnying laugh and ran faster.

But the snowfairies moved as fast as the wind, and they were dancing with the snowflakes, far faster than a little stuffed unicorn, even a magically awakened stuffed unicorn. More, forgetting their task, they moved higher and higher in the snowstorm, leaving Merry farther and farther behind. And before too long, she was alone on the road.

The snow was deepening as it fell faster and faster, making Merry slower and slower. The cars driving by seemed bigger and scarier with their loud noises and whooshing tires. Sometimes she was even blown over by the wind from some of the biggest trucks.

Even so, Merry picked herself up and kept moving.

Eileen misses me, and I miss her. I'll keep going until I find her.

The sun was just peeking up over the horizon when Merry heard a quiet whoosh behind her. She thought it was more of the big cars and trucks and so she didn't pay it much mind. Until she looked over her shoulder and saw that it was drifting off the road and coming right at her.

Merry jumped forward and began running as fast as she could. She knew that if those big tires ran over her, she would be squished flat!

Suddenly, when she thought she could run no more, something grabbed her from above and she went flying sideways up into the air, just missing the hood of the car. She looked in the windshield and saw a young man with wide eyes as he jerked the car back onto the road. The car stopped with a sideways slide, and the young man's mouth opened wider than his eyes as he stared at the strange sight of a flying unicorn.

Merry looked up to see what had grabbed her and saved her from the road.

At first, she saw only brown and tan feathers and big wings flapping nearly silently on the wind. Snow was still swirling around, though far less than had been earlier. A head craned down to peer at Merry for a moment, and she realized an owl had grabbed her up. Along with that came the thought that she was so lucky that the owl had saved her and that she was moving much faster now.

"Thank you, owl for saving me!"

The owl peered down at her again, but didn't reply.

The sun coming up was very beautiful, as it was the first time that Merry had seen ta sunrise. She blinked at the brightness and enjoyed the pinks and purples in the clouds that nearly matched her own mane and tail. It was so pretty.

The sun's rays were warm even in the wind's cold and reminded Merry of the hugs that Eileen would give her as they snuggled under the blankets, warm and dry.

The owl still hadn't spoken to her when they started coming lower into the trees. Some of the leaves and twigs started brushing against Merry, and she started moving her legs to pretend that she was running on the treetops. White from the snow and dark green where the Christmas trees grew down below. They landed with a thump in a nest of sticks and feathers. There was another owl there waiting.

"Oh! You brought me home to visit your family," Merry smiled up at the owl that had carried her. Both of the owls stared at her, big yellow eyes reflecting Merry's bright blue ones.

The second owl turned its head all the way upside down, and Merry tried to do the same thing, and when the owl turned her head the other way, Merry did that too.

"Whoo," the owl spoke then.

"I'm Merry! Nice to meet you. I'm going to find my girl, Eileen. The snowfairies say that she misses me very much, and I miss her too. Thank your husband for me please for the ride."

The two owls looked at each other for a moment, and then the wife owl quickly reached out with her beak and plucked two hairs from Merry's mane. Then she tucked it into the nest with the soft feathers. She wove the blue and purple in with the white and tan and brown. It looked very festive.

"I'm glad you like my hair, but I really need to be moving on. I have to find Eileen."

The husband owl turned around in the nest and launched out into the shadowy forest, where the sun had not yet touched the depths.

Merry gave a little bow, touching her horn to her outstretched hoof, and then she too jumped out of the nest.

She was about halfway down to the ground when she remembered she didn't have wings to fly. So she ran and ran as fast as she could, bouncing from one branch to another. She passed a startled family of squirrels. A beautiful red cardinal was awakened by her running, and he flew off, rustling leaves and shaking snow off the branches.

And with one last very big jump, she was on the ground.

"Well now, wasn't that fun!" Merry exclaimed. Then she started trotting to find a way out of the forest. She was a little muddier, and with some twigs and leaves in her tail, but it was time to find Eileen.

Merry had just come out of the trees and into a meadow when she heard a strange sound. Like someone sniffing very loudly. The snow and frost had already melted from the sunshine, leaving the grasses and ground in all different shades of gold and brown.

Merry turned around as the snuffling got louder just in time to see a big golden dog with very white teeth scoop her softly into its mouth and start running across the meadow.

"Whee!" Merry said. After the first few moments of worry, she realized the dog's teeth were barely even touching her. While it was a little wet, they were moving in great running jumps and they were across the wide meadow in no time at all. Merry thought that surely the dog was taking her straight to Eileen.

Well, that sped things up!

But instead of a sweet, dark-haired girl with brown eyes, the dog dropped Merry at the feet of a boy with hair the same color as the dog. The boy's dark brown eyes shone when he looked down at Merry.

"What'cha got, boy?" He spoke to the dog, who wagged his tail and picked Merry back up again in his mouth, handing her to the boy. Merry started to ask him if he would take her to see Eileen. But before the words could even begin, the boy took her from the dog.

"Ah, an old stuffy. You probably shouldn't be playing with that, Sam," the boy said as he cocked his arm back and launched Merry into the sky and across the grassy bank.

Merry's legs windmilled in the air trying to right herself as she somersaulted through the air, coming down onto crackly grass and rolling onto soft moss and sand. She had no time to right herself as the dog, Sam, grabbed her back up again and ran straight back to the boy. She was sure that this was not the best way to get back to Eileen.

The boy took her and launched her again and again until she was completely dizzy and didn't know up from down or side from side. Each time Sam would grab her and run back to the boy. But he was never unkind with his sharp teeth, for which Merry was thankful.

And then it happened.

Instead of landing on the sand and moss, she landed with a splash.

She was pulled out, toward the center of the river, and moved downstream in the current. She heard the boy call Sam back.

"Don't get in the river, Sam, it's too cold. Get back here, I've got a good stick for you."

As Merry spun around in the eddy, she saw the dog at the shore watch her for a moment and then turn and run off to meet with the boy again. And then she was trying to swim off to the shore, hooves not really made for swimming, weighing her down until her head was barely above the water.

Well, at least I'm moving pretty fast. I hope Eileen is okay without me.

It was nearing sundown, and Merry was still in the water.

She had managed to grab hold of a branch that was floating along in the water, so she wasn't so tired from swimming. Merry was enjoying the sparkle of the sun upon the water. She saw bits of snow and ice still clinging to a few of the shadows along the bank, and they were pretty, too.

Merry saw a man was sitting near the bank on a stump and he had a stick in his hand. He would take the long stick and wave it around, sometimes behind him and sometimes in front.

When she got closer, he waved the stick at her, and suddenly Merry was caught by a hook that yanked her off the log and drew her across the water. The old man grabbed the part of the line that was holding the hook and raised Merry up to eye level.

He shook his head.

"Well, some kind of horsey, I guess. I'll take you home to the Mrs."

He took out the hook that was tangled in Merry's mane and set Merry on the ground behind him.

Merry's legs were wobbly from being in the water so long, and so it took her quite a while to stand up. When she did, most of the water had run off, so she only had to shake a little bit. But now her fur was standing straight out, and her mane and tail were really tangled.

The old man caught one more fish. He put it into a bucket, closed up his fishing tackle box, and wound up the line on his fishing pole. He picked up Merry and put her under one arm and then picked up his bucket, box, and pole with the other. He trudged his way up the bank and to his old rusty truck that was parked on the side of the road.

The old man put the fishing things in the back of the truck, and he put Merry on the passenger seat.

It was dark when they pulled up to the old man's tiny cottage with blue and white faded paint. He picked up Merry and put her under his arm again after parking. He got out of the truck and took the fishing gear from the back.

He went around the side of the house and hung his pole on the wall under the carport and placed the tackle box on a shelf. He left the bucket with water and the fish sitting there and opened the side door to go into the little kitchen.

The kitchen was warm, and while it was faded too, it had been decorated with love.

Bright pink gingham curtains, clean white counters, and a shiny sink were on one wall. There was a heavy wooden table that was lovingly polished, and matching gingham placemats sat in front of each polished wooden chair.

On the stove, a warm pot of soup was boiling gently. There were also biscuits in the oven, and it filled the kitchen with the aroma of lovely baking food Merry could smell.

An older woman came around the corner from another room. She wore a cheerful pink apron, and her smile lit up her face when she saw Merry and the little old man. She was so pretty with her soft white hair curled like the clouds Merry had seen that day. Her blue eyes were almost the same color as Merry's.

"What did you find, dear?" the old woman asked sweetly.

"Some white horsey in the water. Got caught in my fishing line."

"Well let's put it in the sink and get you some dinner." The old woman took Merry from him and placed her in the sink. She bustled about to set the table and serve dinner for the little old man. Love and familiarity were in every movement.

After dinner, the little old man went through the doorway into the other room. The old woman tidied up the kitchen and then picked Merry up to take a closer look.

"I think with a bath and brushing, my dear, that you will clean up nicely. I know there is some little girl that would love to have you for a Christmas present. I'll get you cleaned up and then take you to the thrift shop tomorrow."

Merry didn't want to go to a thrift shop, and she already had a little girl who wanted her. But a bath and brushing would be very nice. Merry decided she would tell the little old lady about Eileen tomorrow. Maybe the little old lady would help her find Eileen.

The soapy bubble bath was warm, and the little old lady's hands were soft. And by the time she was being dried in front of a warm fire, Merry was asleep.

When Merry woke up, she was in the front seat of a car again.

The little old lady was driving this time. She wore a denim-blue jacket and a cheerful scarf around her neck. But her hair was just as white and curly as the night before. The little old lady was humming a Christmas song as she drove. Merry hummed quietly along.

Merry was too short to see out the window, so she was surprised when the car came to a stop. The little old lady turned the car off and then picked up Merry from her seat and rubbed noses with her.

"You are so pretty now, I'm sure someone will buy you right away."

Merry had fallen asleep before she had a chance to talk to the little old lady about finding Eileen. But she didn't have a chance to do so now either. The little old lady opened the door and carried her briskly into the shop.

The shop smelled of old and new altogether. But it was brightly decorated with Christmas lights and strings of garland, with red and gold ornaments hanging from them. The little old lady sat Merry in the very front window, right under a Christmas tree that was decorated with a star on top.

Merry watched as the lady straightened the desk and checked the aisles. She turned on more lights as she went, and soon there was the smell of cinnamon and pine drifting on the air.

Merry turned to watch as people began passing by on the sidewalk. She even saw a little girl press her nose against the window and stare excitedly at her. That caused Merry to carefully back away under the tree and hide behind a large decorated present. The store was busy all day, and Merry never did have a chance to talk to the old lady. But the old lady was always kind and cheerful, humming along with the Christmas music. She also gave candy canes to the small children who came in with their parents.

Sunset was coming, and thankfully no one had noticed Merry hiding under the tree. The little old lady was closing down the shop. She turned off the lights, and she turned off the Christmas music. She seemed to have forgotten all about Merry.

So when the little old lady put on her jacket, and gathered up her purse, Merry took her chance.

She jumped out of the window and hid in the shadows right by the door. When the little old lady opened the door, Merry quickly slipped outside. Merry then ran down the sidewalk and around the corner, where she hid behind a trashcan until the little old lady's car drove off.

Merry stepped to the edge of the alley that she had hidden in and looked out at the street. There were cars driving by swiftly, and people walking swiftly as well. Everyone seemed to be in a hurry.

The sun had gone down behind some of the tall buildings, and the Christmas lights and streetlights were coming on. Merry loved to watch the glow of the lights and stood there for quite a while. Finally, she decided she needed to move on if she was going to find Eileen.

She looked to the left, and she looked to the right; so many buildings and people in cars. Merry just didn't know which way she needed to go. Then she heard some music.

Merry decided she would head toward the music, and maybe that would help her find Eileen.

Once she was out on the sidewalk, people were moving very quickly, kicking their feet and nearly kicking Merry. So she moved just off the edge of the sidewalk, but not into the road where the cars were. Unfortunately, it was very muddy and wet there, and even some ice remained, so she slipped and slid and got very muddy again.

Would Eileen even recognize me?

There were so many lights on the street and lights in the various shops' windows that Merry couldn't see any stars in the sky. Finally, she came to the place where she had heard the music. There were lots and lots of people gathered together wearing thick coats and gloves and boots, standing nearly shoulder to shoulder. She tried to work her way through them so that she could see who was making the music. She got bumped and stepped on a few times but finally made it through.

There was a group of children, some of them dressed in white with wings, which reminded her of the snowfairies; others were in colorful clothes and were gathered around a wooden box with a doll wrapped in it. More children were on each side dressed in coats and gloves and hats, and they were the ones singing. They reminded Merry so much of Eileen.

As more people arrived and others left, Merry got shoved further and further to the side until she was nearly under a bush. She sat there for a long time just listening, until all the people started leaving, and the children stopped singing.

Merry didn't know which way to go, and the warm voices singing somehow made her even sadder once they were gone. The noise of the cars had quieted, and Merry felt very alone.

"I do not think I will ever find Eileen again." Merry felt something warm and wet sliding down her cheeks and brushed off a tear with her hoof.

It was just too much for a little unicorn all by herself.

With her head bowed, and her mane and forelock covering her face, it was quite some time before Merry noticed that there were snowflakes falling on her. She finally stood up and shook herself all over before she walked out from under the bush. The snow was falling much heavier. Merry noticed the falling snow was colored from all the Christmas lights. Green and red, yellow and blue—and they sparkled just like the light did.

Forgetting to be sad for a moment, Merry started running around trying to catch one of the snowflakes with her horn. A snowfairy appeared in front of her and just like that, was gone again. Merry looked around to see if she could find where it went. FeatherSnow flew down in front of her and spoke.

"There you are! Hurry along now! We don't have a lot of time."

"I can't run as fast as you, you will have to go slower. Or maybe you could ride on my horn and show me the way?" Merry was excited to have found the snowfairies and didn't want to lose them again.

"Okay I can do that," said FeatherSnow. "But it's a long way to go, so I will ask some of the other snowfairies to help."

FeatherSnow flew off and soon was back with over a dozen snowfairies. They grabbed onto Merry's mane and tail and the fur along her back.

"Now you must run as if you're running on the snowflakes, fast and light." FeatherSnow settled on Merry's horn, holding on as though she was riding it.

Merry began running, thinking about when she ran in the forest, on the branches, the twigs and the leaves. She remembered how happy she had been. She remembered when the dog was carrying her, how fast she went. She remembered when the owl carried her how quiet it was. And she remembered the kindness of the little old man and little old woman. She lifted higher in the air and went fasterand faster. The snowfairies directed her the way she needed to go.

Soon, it seemed, they were coming down in the yard of a tiny house. The door with a holly wreath on it opened as they landed, and a young woman came out. Merry was a little disappointed because it was not Eileen or Eileen's mother.

"You must be Merry," the young woman said. Her voice was cheerful, and her smile was bright. "Eileen misses you very much. But we can't send you back looking the way you do right now. Come on in and we'll get you cleaned up. I think we can have you ready for Christmas morning."

The red-haired young woman held the door open a little further. The snowfairies flew off as the woman waved goodbye to them. She motioned for Merry to come in. Merry was surprised; no one else seemed to pay her much attention. So she trotted on into the house. The house was clean and cozy, and reminded Merry of the little old woman's house.

"You wait over by the fire while I get a brush and make you a bath. We still have a couple of hours until morning. You got here just in time." The young woman turned and began making preparations just as she had said.

Merry headed over to the fire, but not too close, as she could see the little firefairies dancing in the flames. Things moved quickly after that. Merry was bathed and dried and brushed. Little red and green Christmas bows were braided in her mane and tail. The young woman, who told Merry her name was Noelle, also gave her a little plaid horse blanket that was just her size.

They finished everything up just as the sun was rising. Noelle picked Merry up and held her in her arms. She wrapped the shawl around both of them and out the door they went.

Noelle walked around the fence, down the sidewalk and up to another door with a simple red bow on it. Noelle sat Merry down on the stoop and then rang the doorbell. It took a moment, but then Merry heard footsteps, and the door opened. First she saw Eileen's mother, and that made her little hooves dance.

But behind Eileen's mother, Merry saw Eileen!

Noelle and Eileen's mother were speaking about something, but Merry only had eyes for Eileen. Then Eileen saw Merry.

Eileen came running right out past her mother and scooped Merry up into her arms and hugged her so tight. Merry was so happy she thought she was going to burst into a thousand sparkles.

"Mom! It's Merry, she came back, she found me!"

Christmas Day had been lovely, with the family, presents and good food. Their neighbor, Noelle, had come over with fresh pumpkin pie to share. Eileen had kept Merry right by her side through it all. Eileen had gone to sleep without crying that night, hugging her old friend, Merry, and thinking that making new friends like Noelle and maybe other friends at school might not be so bad after all.

Merry crept out of bed once Eileen was asleep. She had been in a kind of sleep, herself, most of the day, but knew that her girl, Eileen, was happy. Merry was very happy herself. She jumped up on the windowsill and looked out at the snow falling softly. She could see the little snowfairies dancing between the snowflakes, playing games.

Merry looked down at Noelle's house, with lights all around in the windows, and saw Noelle walk outside her back door and look up at the window in which Merry stood, and wave. Merry gave a little bow, touching her horn to her hoof, and then standing and giving her a wink.

Then Merry very happily went back to bed. Love had brought her home.

A Fae-ry Merry Christmas

By Lydia Sherrer

[This story is one of the *Lily Singer Adventures* in Lydia Sherrer's *Love, Lies and Hocus Pocus* universe.]

"I thought hangin' out with you two was gonna be excitin'. Why am I stuck puttin' popcorn on string?"

"It's a Christmas gift for our fae friends, Jamie, that's why," said Lily primly, ignoring her teenage brother's exaggerated sigh from across the farmhouse table. She'd been unsure about including him, since he'd only started studying wizard magic recently. But free labor was nothing to sneeze at. They had *a lot* of popcorn to string. "You can't have fun without a little work, so stop complaining and keep stringing."

"I thought the fae were scary, powerful beings of pure magic that we were supposed to avoid? I mean, Mom 'bout tanned my hide the other day when she caught me callin' Gavi to take a peek at my report card before she gets it from school."

"And you wonder why you aren't supposed to call on the fae," Sebastian muttered, shaking his head. Lily wondered if the witch now regretted introducing Jamie to his fae allies—her brother seemed to have zero sense of self preservation. "Look, kid. They aren't malicious—at least most of them aren't. But they aren't nice either. They're not pets, friends, or even wild animals."

"They are too friends!" Lily protested.

"Okay, yeah, maybe for *you*. But you've got a soft spot for them and they know it. They can't help themselves. It's puppy love." He gave her a big, goofy, fond grin that made her roll her eyes.

"It is nothing of the sort. I'm *polite* and *respectful*. Unlike a certain *witch* I know."

"Hey, the fae love my roguish charm."

"Yuki does, maybe. But only because he makes just as much trouble as you."

"Sure, but he still likes it. The point, kid, is that the fae aren't beings you can mess around with. I'll bet Gavi would have bargained with you to leave the kitchen window open for him, then what would your mother have done to you after a giant fae raven ransacked your kitchen and broke everything because you invited him in? You need smarts *and* wisdom to deal with the fae, and you ain't got either."

"Hey!"

"Don't take it as an insult. You're young. You'll get there. But you can start by not thinking the fae are errand boys who will help you escape your mom's wrath for your bad grades."

Jamie was inclined to grumble, and shot dark looks at both of them as they worked on their garlands.

Further argument was forestalled by Freda, Lily and Jamie's mother, bustling into the kitchen with two big bags of shiny red apples. The rest of the Singers were out looking after farm business. The mundane members of the family thought they were making a "treat tree" for the local wildlife, something Tom Singer, the patriarch of the family, scratched his head at, considering the lengths he went to keep "varmints" away from the vegetable garden and grain supply. But he humored Lily and Sebastian all the same.

It wasn't that Lily's mundane family members didn't know about magic—they'd been reluctantly and unhappily dragged into Lily and Freda's world a time or two. It simply couldn't be helped. But Lily had decided they would feel more comfortable if they weren't going to sleep at night worrying what sorts of magical denizens of the fae realm were rollicking around their farm.

Jamie, of course, would have pitched a fit if they'd tried to exclude him, despite his questionable decision-making capabilities, so his wizard mother had reluctantly agreed to let him help. After all, this was his world as much as Freda and Lily's, and he had to learn eventually.

"Remind me why we're puttin' bottles of bourbon in the caramel sauce?" Jamie asked, looking askance at the oven top.

"Makes the pixies happy," Sebastian said distractedly, tongue sticking out the side of his mouth as he tried to poke the large, twine-threaded needle through the flexible shell of the peanut he held between two fingers. He was alternating between peanuts and grapes on his string, while Lily helped Jamie with the popcorn.

"But why alcohol?"

"Beats me," Sebastian said with a shrug. "It's not just the pixies who like it, though the little buggers are the ones that go bonkers for it. I've caught Gavi drinking straight out of my shot glass like it was water, the big feathery thief. I think it might be to them like sugar is to us—a nice little endorphin rush. I've never seen them show much interest in refined sugar, though I've offered candy often enough. Some go for food sweetened with natural sugars like honey, but that's it."

"That's why I made my own dipping sauce using honey instead of cane sugar," Freda said, stirring the slowly bubbling pot full of golden goo. Several empty bottles of bourbon and one empty bottle of rum sat on the counter beside the pot. "Now, who wants to help me dip apples?"

Jamie's hand shot up.

"Me!"

His mother's eyes narrowed.

"You are *not* allowed to lick the apples, young man. You are not yet eighteen, and these treats are for the fae, not *you*."

"I won't, cross my heart," Jamie said, his shit-eating grin suspiciously undimmed.

Lily gave him a sideways look. Likely he planned to lick his fingers, or the spoon, or something else besides the apples. But she left it to their mother to deal with. He wasn't *her* child, thank the heavens. She would never have had the patience for him, reprobate that he was. A lot like Sebastian, come to think of it. Her gaze shifted to her boyfriend and she couldn't stop the smile from sliding across her face. His tongue was still sticking out the side of his mouth as he worked. It was so adorable she wanted to pinch his cheek. She could only imagine the sorts of mischief Sebastian and Jamie would have gotten up to if they'd been teenagers together.

The world might never have recovered.

Thankfully, Sebastian had come by some hard-won sense since his teenage years. And hopefully between her, Sebastian, Freda, and Madam Barrington, they could teach Jamie enough sense to keep him from the sorts of tragic and heart-wrenching life lessons Sebastian had gotten himself tangled up in at that age.

Hopefully.

"Now, Jamie, what's the proper way to address a fae, and why do you use it?" Sebastian said, drilling the young man as they worked.

"*Elwa* and their true name. *Elwa* 'cuz it shows respect, and their true name 'cuz it's connected to their essence and they can hear it anywhere in the world."

"Right. And do they *have* to respond when you call their name?"

"Nope."

"Correct. They'll ignore you if you tick them off, if they aren't interested in bargaining, if they're busy, or for any number of other reasons. So what do you do if you call and there's no response."

"Uhhhh, try again?"

"Maybe. Persistence has its benefits. Patience does, too. Sometimes they wait to see how much you want them, just to mess with you. Yuki is a big fan of that tactic. He's a bushy-tailed reprobate and proud of it."

"Says the kettle calling the pot black," Lily said archly.

"Hey! I'm not a *bushy-tailed* reprobate, I'm a devilishly handsome, impressively-statured reprobate." He flashed her a smoldering grin, and she looked away before it could make her blush.

Nope, too late.

"Ew, you two are gross," Jamie whined.

Sebastian leaned over his chair and punched the young man lightly in the arm where he was standing holding apples to give to Freda.

"Don't even start, young'un. You'd be flat out lying if you tried to say you weren't interested in girls. I've seen the way you drool when Mallory is around and you think she isn't looking."

"*Gross*! Dude, I'm *related* to her."

"No, actually, you're not. Not by blood and not even by marriage."

"Oh...well fine, but it's still weird. And anyway, she would skewer me if I even talked to her, much less asked her out."

"Yup, she absolutely would," Sebastian agreed with good-natured glee.

"Less jawing and more apples, Jamie," Freda said sternly. Jamie started and Lily hid a grin. Her little brother had been staring vacantly at the wall, and Lily wondered how bad his crush on Mallory really was.

Poor Jamie.

Poor *Mallory*.

"Just keep the apples coming, honey. Once I fill up this cookie sheet you can go tie the dogs up, then set it out on the porch to cool so the caramel can set. Lily, sweetie, I assume I don't have to worry about Sir Kipling licking them if we leave them unguarded?"

"They'll be safe," Lily said, giggling at the picture of her cat Sir Kipling with sticky caramel smeared across his dignified whiskers. "If it's not meat or a dairy product, he turns up his nose."

"Where *is* Sir Kipling, anyway?" Freda asked, looking around. "I'm surprised he's not here supervising."

"Asleep on my bed, I think. He said to wake him once things 'got interesting.' Apparently stringing popcorn isn't worthy of his personalized attention."

"Oh, he'll come running once we start calling fae," Sebastian snickered. "He loves watching them, even if he knows he can't chase them."

"Well, then," Lily said, "let's get back to work so that our glorious overlord doesn't wither away from boredom."

Being the biggest and strongest, Sebastian was assigned the five-gallon bucket of caramel-covered apples to carry. Jamie had the basket full of popcorn garland and Freda had the one of peanuts and grapes. They'd drizzled the leftover caramel across the garlands, making them messy to handle. Freda had caught Jamie licking his hands more than once, but eventually gave up scolding him. It wasn't as if fae could catch germs from humans.

The "treat" making had taken longer than anticipated, and evening came early in December, so the overcast sky was already getting dark by the time they set off through the brisk December air. It was colder than they were used to in the south. Not freezing, but close, though at least there was no precipitation. Lily was bundled up in two coats, gloves, hat, and scarf. Sebastian was decked out in a mis-matched assortment of odds and ends he'd borrowed from Drew on top of his leather coat, while Freda was wrapped in a well-loved quilted coat she'd made herself. Jamie, oddly, didn't seem to mind the cold, and wore only a light jacket.

As for Sir Kipling, his thick coat made him immune to the chill. Lily felt sure he had Maine Coon or Norwegian Forest cat in his ancestry, but had no idea what his dam and sire looked like since she'd adopted him off the street as a kitten. The underbrush he picked his way through now slid across his silky fur, finding no purchase as he followed after them like the lithe hunter he was.

Jamie led the way, since he knew the farm better than anyone else. Freda had asked him to find an evergreen bush or tree with strong enough branches to hold the treats, but still low enough that they could reach without a ladder. Jamie led them along a fence row, through a field, and to the woods following the creek behind the farmhouse. There he slowed and examined the trees he had to choose from, finally settling on a young cedar tree that was only about a dozen feet tall with plenty of sturdy branches to hang their offerings from.

They got to work while Sir Kipling supervised from under a nearby juniper bush. Before it had gotten much dimmer, the tree was covered in lopsided garlands and dozens of apples as high up as they could reach.

Their hands were also covered in caramel.

"Well, I'll admit I might have gone a bit lighter on the caramel," Freda said, looking doubtfully at her hands. Jamie, of course, was already licking his. Lily made a disgusted face at the sight. What was it with teenage boys?

"Aw, don't worry about it, the fae will clean 'em for you," Sebastian said, chortling. "Just hold them out and stay still. Everybody ready?"

"As ready as I'll ever be," Freda murmured, looking apprehensive.

"Don't worry, Mother. The animal aspects are really very sweet. Don't let their looks intimidate you."

"I think they like women better than men," Sebastian said, grumpily. "Even though *I'm* the one who gives them alcohol. It's totally unfair. Lily, you might as well do the honors."

Lily cocked her head, a smile tucked into the corners of her mouth.

"No, I think you should do it. The treat tree was your idea, after all. And besides, you know them better than I do. You know the best ones to invite who will actually enjoy all this."

"Oh. Okay. Good idea." His smile was broad and bright, and Lily returned it in kind.

She didn't bother listening closely as the exotic fae language began rolling off Sebastian's tongue like honey. She'd heard it all before. Jamie, though, was riveted, eyes wide and wondrous as Sebastian called, teased, complimented, and cajoled. The teenager even jumped when the first pixie showed up—Pip, unsurprisingly. She had a nose for alcohol and wasn't about to pass up an opportunity for free food.

But she was only the first.

Sebastian told her to spread the word and tell all the local low fae that a feast was being served, and she wasn't too thrilled with it. Greedy little bugger, as Sebastian often called her. But with a firm promise that he would save the best treats for her, she finally vanished again and soon fairy lights began to appear in the darkening night like winter fireflies, creeping cautiously along branches and through the tall, dry grass.

Lily wasn't sure what the sight looked like to Jamie or Freda, since she could see through the basic fae glamour that they used to stay hidden from humans. But based on Jamie's eyes widening to the size of saucers, at least some of them must have dropped their glamour once they felt reassured by Sebastian's presence.

Of course, if they'd known better, they might have thought to be a bit more cautious. When Lily glanced at the juniper bush, she found Sir Kipling crouched there, yellow eyes wide and pupils hugely dilated, reflecting the flitting, multicolored lights. His head twitched this way and that as he tracked their movements, though he seemed to have suppressed the instinctive meowing "chatter" he always made at birds and squirrels he spotted outside Lily's apartment windows.

He knew he wasn't allowed to chase pixies, and had apparently dredged up enough self-control over his feline instincts to remain stationary even when presented with such a smorgasbord of tantalizing targets.

Apparently her cat was a masochist.

Soon enough Pip was back and joined the descending flurry of fae on the cedar tree. In no time the tree looked like a true Christmas tree, covered in fluttering, darting lights of all colors. Lily saw the branches of the cedar quivering down near the ground, and spotted a wrinkled little grey hand shooting out to wrench juicy grapes off the garland string. Apparently Grimmold the mold fae liked more than just aged pizza, at least if it was drizzled with alcohol-laced caramel.

Then the animal aspects started arriving.

Lily's smile broadened and she lifted her head in greeting as two gigantic, elk-like forms stepped silently into the human realm, materializing like phantoms glowing softly in the dusk. They easily stood six to seven feet high at the shoulders, and their antlers spread wide from their heads. One stood about a foot higher than the other, and its antlers were thicker and more gnarled.

Freda yelped in surprise when she caught sight of them.

"*Elwa* Zarim, Zaril," Lily said with a small bow. "It is good to see you again. Are you doing well?"

"*As well as can be expected, shining one. And who is this?*" Zaril said to their minds in the way that the animal aspects did, stretching her neck out to sniff Freda's bangs. Her mental voice was deep, but sweet, like a nightingale.

Lily's mother stood absolutely still, frozen with an expression of terrified wonder on her face. Jamie had a nearly identical look, and Lily tried to remember if this was the first time they'd spoken with fae mind to mind before. They'd had so many adventures and misadventures, sometimes it was hard to keep track.

"Oh, This is my mother," Lily responded belatedly. "She made caramel apples for you. It was Sebastian's idea, though. Would you like a taste? Hold up your hands, Mother. You don't have to be afraid. These are the aspect of Horned King, the ruler of the forest."

Freda hesitated, but then followed Lily's prompting, and Zaril sniffed at the sticky hands. The fae snorted in amusement, making Freda jump.

"I smell nectar of the field. The witch knows us too well. Thank you, shining mother, for your gift." And with that the fae's long, rough tongue stretched out and began licking Freda's hands clean.

"Oh! Oh! That's-that's q-quite all right," Lily's poor mother tried to say. But by the time she'd gotten her wits and voice back, Zaril had already made short work of the sticky hands and turned to lick Lily's as she offered them. Then the giant fae wandered over to the cedar tree where she joined her duality in crunching down on juicy apples.

"What manner of bargain is this? Is this?" said a bright, sharp mental voice in Lily's head, accompanied by a deep croak and a flapping of wings.

Gavi, one half the aspect of Raven and as nosey as they came, landed on Zarim's antlers and cocked his head at the humans.

"No bargain, old friend. Just a gift." Sebastian had shoved his gloved hands under his armpits but still managed to look casual about it, even with his face half hidden by a scarf. "It's something we humans do this time of year, for the people we care about. And I care about you all, so..." he shrugged, and while his stance was still casual, Lily could see the stiffness in his shoulders.

"Getting soft, you are, human. Soon we fae will not know what to do with you. What to do with you!"

"I'm sure you'll figure it out," Sebastian said with a grin, shoulders relaxing. "It won't kill you to face a little uncertainty every now and then. It keeps life interesting."

A second giant Raven faded into the dusk and alighted on Zaril's antlers.

"Anything to keep him occupied! He is forever croaking about boring this and boring that. Now he may take his own medicine. His own medicine!"

Gali, Gavi's other half, gave a perfunctory croak and hopped from antler to antler until she could flutter down onto Lily's shoulder. The giant raven took up all the room available and Lily had to tilt her head to accommodate her. Once settled, the raven aspect poked her beak at Lily's hat until Lily reluctantly removed it so the enthusiastic fae could run her beak through Lily's hair bun in a vain attempt to groom her. Lily bore it patiently, not bothering to point out, as always, that Gali was making more of a mess, not less.

"Yes, yes, thank you, Gali. My hair looks very nice, now. Why don't you go enjoy some apples? Sebastian scattered some on the ground over there for the smaller fae."

Gali rattled in approval and hopped to the ground, stabbing at the nearest piece of fruit with a huge black beak that split the entire apple in two.

"*If you're not careful you'll spoil the low fae,*" a dry, faintly mocking mental voice said, and Lily craned her head to see where Yuki was hiding. She spotted the silver fae fox beneath the same juniper bush as Sir Kipling, and the cat looked none too pleased about the company. "*They'll be following you around like hungry puppies before long if you keep giving them food willy nilly without making them work for it.*"

"Aw, come on, lighten up, Yuki," Sebastian said. "It's Christmas. Even wild animals get a bounty from nature every now and then."

"*I care not what you do, witch. I just thought you'd like to know you'll have only yourself to blame when pixies start waking you up in the middle of the night, searching your pockets for grapes and peanuts. You know they have no concept of personal boundaries.*"

Sebastian scowled at that, and Lily wondered if he was remembering the pixies in the shower episode.

"Come, Yuki, leave poor Sebastian alone. Why don't you try an apple? I hear foxes love apples."

"*Hmm, don't mind if I do, oh radiant one.*" And with that the fox got up to start nosing through the grass.

Gavi, who was still sitting in Zarim's antlers and turning his head this way and that as he examined the humans, finally gave a perfunctory croak and launched himself off the majestic fae to flap his way down onto Sebastian's leather-encased shoulder. Sebastian bore the weight without comment, though he leaned away when the raven pecked lightly at his hat.

"I am *not* taking off my hat so you can mess up my hair. Do you even realize how cold it is? I'll freeze to death!"

"*Spoilsport, you are. But who is this with you, now? This is a youngling. A youngling!*"

"Yes, exactly. This is Jamie, and he's a *kid*, so don't go making bargains with him. He's still learning what's what."

Jamie's expression went from wide-eyed to mulish and he crossed his arms. The raven gave a cackling rattle at the sight.

"*Act like a youngling, be treated like a youngling. That is the way of things. The way of things!*"

That seemed to make an impression on Jamie, because he slowly uncrossed his arms, his brow furrowing in thought.

"*Rush not the seasons of growth, youngling, for they are bought at great cost. Greater age requires greater sacrifice. Be wary and wise in what you wish for. What you wish for!*"

No one else spoke. Everyone seemed to be digesting the raven's words while watching the gathered fae feast on the bountiful gift. More animals had shown up: a fierce-looking boar the size of a small pony with curved, sharp tusks nosed at the base of the cedar with relaxed movements, completely ignoring the humans; a rotund raccoon-like creature that looked as cute as could be, until you noticed that it was as big as a dog; a pair of shining silver squirrels that chattered at each other as they devoured peanuts in the upper branches of the cedar, pausing only to shoo away the pixies that contended for space on the now-crowded branches.

Abruptly, Jamie bowed at the waist and addressed Gavi.

"Thanks for your advice, *Gahravvi'arak*. I'll remember it."

"*See that you do, youngling. And Merry Christmas, as you humans say, no? Merry Christmas!*"

"Yeah, that's what we say," Jamie confirmed with a grin. "Merry Christmas."

After that, Gavi lost interest in the humans and hopped off Sebastian's shoulder to join his duality pecking at apples on the leaf-covered ground. Lily scooted over to Sebastian and tucked herself under one of his arms as they watched the enchanting site. The evening had darkened toward night, and the fae shone pale and ghostly in the gathering gloom, their faint luminescence reflecting off the leaves and branches around them to give the whole area a particularly festive feel.

"Hey you," Sebastian murmured, making the motion to plant a kiss on the top of her head, though his scarf got in the way. "Thanks for helping."

"It was fun, if a little...sticky," Lily said. She felt more than heard him chuckle.

"Just be glad I didn't ask you to help me give gifts to the carnivorous fae. How are you with a butcher's knife?"

Lily shuddered.

"I'll pass, thanks."

"Honestly most of the carnivores would probably enjoy this, too," he said, a grin in his voice. "I just didn't want to scare your mom and Jamie. The meat-eaters are a bit less...civilized."

"You weren't worried about scaring *me*?"

"Are you kidding? You'd probably have them on their backs begging you for tummy rubs in no time."

Lily elbowed him.

"Hey, guys," Jamie muttered out of the side of his mouth, stepping close to Sebastian to speak quietly, though his eyes were fixed on the fae. He must not have noticed the two of them snuggling, or he would have been making exaggerated retching sounds. "I thought all the stories said to never thank a fae. Doesn't that, like, put you in their debt or something?"

"There's debt, and then there's debt," Sebastian murmured back, his stance relaxed. "The debt of friendship is worth the cost. But it takes two to tango."

"Okaaay," Jamie said. "What the heck does *that* mean?"

"It means," Lily said, "that you should be careful who you give your trust to."

"So...who *can* I give my trust to?" the young man pressed.

"Figuring that out is part of growing up," Sebastian offered unhelpfully. "But you can start by watching your elders and not repeating their mistakes."

"Right. So don't become a 'Professional Witch' and expect to actually make money."

Sebastian swatted Jamie across the back of the head.

"Ow!"

"You deserved that, youngling," Lily said with a straight face as their mother hid a smile behind her hand.

"My professional witch business made plenty of money, I'll have you know, when my clients actually paid me. My problem wasn't my business model, it was my soft heart."

CAN WE STOP TALKING ABOUT BORING THINGS AND GO BACK TO THE HOUSE? Gold letters floated up from beneath the juniper bush, the result of Sir Kipling's enchanted collar that enabled the familiar to communicate with humans. Sir Kipling's dark gray head, invisible in the darkness if not for his white markings, turned to fix baleful yellow eyes on Lily.

*ALL THESE DELECTABLE—I MEAN DELIGHTFUL—FAE
ARE MAKING ME HUNGRY. YOU DID GET ME SALMON
WHEN YOU BOUGHT ALL THOSE APPLES, RIGHT?*

Everyone laughed.

Lily tilted her head up, enjoying one last look at the fae, and felt a tiny prick of wetness settle softly on her cheek. Then another, and another.

"It's snowing," she breathed, eyes going wide as she watched flakes begin to drift silently down among their group, reflecting the soft glow of the gathered fae. It rarely snowed in Alabama, and she'd always treasured the sight, even if the temperatures made it miserable to be outside.

"Great, just what I needed, death by snowflake," Sebastian groaned.

"Don't be ungrateful," Freda scolded, bending to pick up and stack the two baskets they'd used to carry the garlands. "It's Christmas time. Children all over the country beg and hope for a white Christmas."

"They can have it," Sebastian muttered, hunching his shoulders and pulling Lily tighter against him as if she could shield him from the offending flakes.

Freda smiled.

"All right, Mr. Grinch. Let's get you back to the house. I'm sure a bit of hot chocolate would perk you right up."

"Oo! Do you have those little marshmallows?"

"Not anymore, I already ate 'em all," Jamie said nonchalantly.

"*What!* Why you greedy, ungrateful little—" Sebastian lunged for the young man, but Jamie dodged him and took off like a shot through the woods back toward the farmhouse, cackling like a madman. Sebastian sprinted after him in hot pursuit, yelling promises of violence and wedgies when he got hold of the teenager.

Lily looked at her mother, and the two of them burst out laughing.

*IF ANYONE HAS EATEN MY SALMON, I WILL RAIN
DOWN WRATH AND DESTRUCTION UPON THEM TO THE
THIRD AND FOURTH GENERATIONS.*

Sir Kipling's golden letters floated past them at waist level as the feline in question began picking his way back toward warmth and food.

"Nobody wants your raw salmon, Kip," Lily pointed out.

SO YOU DID GET SOME? EXCELLENT. At that, the cat took off at a gallop, following in the wake of the two men.

"What is it with males and food?" Lily asked, shaking her head.

"I don't know, honey, but it's universal, so you'd best get used to it."

They linked arm in arm, but before they left Lily turned to look back at the glowing fae, their shapes obscured by the now swiftly falling snow.

"Merry Christmas, friends," she said softly. Zarim's massive head turned and his soft black eyes met hers, the pixie lights reflecting in them like dozens of tiny stars. He dipped his head, then went back to eating apples.

"Peace and light be upon your path, little one. And do not worry about the youngling. He will learn one way or another, just as you did."

"I hope so," Lily murmured, sharing a look with her mother as they started back toward the house.

"He'll have to survive Sebastian's wrath, first," Freda said, one lip quirking.

"Did he really eat *all* the marshmallows?"

"Only the open pack. I know him too well. I keep the extra bags hidden."

"Should we tell Sebastian?"

"Hmm." Freda cocked her head in thought, and in the silence they could hear distant shouting from the direction of the farmhouse. "No, I don't think so. Not yet, at least. They can both use the exercise."

"I guess it wouldn't be Christmas without ransacked marshmallows and life or death battles in the snow," Lily said, then stuck out her tongue, attempting to catch a snowflake.

"The joys of family, my dear. Merry Christmas."

"Merry Christmas, Mother."

If you enjoyed this short story and want more of Lily, Sebastian, and Sir Kipling, you can follow their escapades in the Lily Singer Adventures, *part of the* Love, Lies, and Hocus Pocus *Universe full of humor and heart, by Lydia Sherrer.*

A Time for Rest

By Aaron Canton

Oakleigh's golden eyes blazed with fiery concentration, just as the holy symbol carved on her forehead burned with actual holy fire, and she ferociously swept her broom back and forth in her massive clay hands. The synagogue was a little cramped for the golem but she didn't pause when she bumped against the pews or even when she scraped her head against the ceiling a mere twelve feet off the ground. She flicked her gaze through a window to the predawn darkness outside and then redoubled her efforts, going so far as to pick up a heavy bench in one bulging arm so she could sweep dust out from under it. *Clean the synagogue*, intoned the orders in her head. *Prepare it for Chanukah.*

But then the first rays of the morning sun washed over Oakleigh through the window. Her body shuddered as her clay liquified and drained inwards to reveal a human frame, and though she tried to keep cleaning, the bench wobbled in her weakening arm and she barely managed to lower it safely. The last remnants of clay vanished under her skin and left behind a lanky sixteen-year-old girl with soft brown hair, freckles, and a smaller but still burning holy symbol on her forehead. She rushed to cover the symbol with the headband she'd stashed in a side room alongside her coat and other clothes, then flopped down on the bench and looked around, only smiling when she couldn't find a single speck of dirt. "Did it," she sighed. "Just in time."

Footsteps sounded from outside and Oakleigh turned as her father walked through the synagogue's front door. "Dad!" Oakleigh said, beaming at the gray-haired rabbi with the scraggly beard and the thick down jacket. He took off his glasses to rub his blue eyes, and she felt a hint of shame that he'd had to rise and drive out so early just to pick her up, but she only said aloud, "What do you think?"

Rabbi Brooks reached his daughter and gave her a hug which she eagerly returned, then made a show of looking around the sanctuary before nodding. "Excellent work as always, Oakleigh. I'm sure Mr. Mecham will be happy to know the synagogue is under such good care." Mecham, who normally handled janitorial work at the synagogue, had left town to celebrate Chanukah with extended family back east. "Let's go home."

Oakleigh waited for Brooks to lock up and then followed him back to his little car. She grimaced upon seeing the thick layer of fresh snow which had blanketed the parking lot and forced her father to park on the street; her last set of orders might not have said anything about shoveling the snow, but if she'd paid better attention to the weather she could have asked her father to add that to the instructions he'd written her. "Dad, I'm sorry I didn't think about the snow—" she began.

But Brooks only gave her a gentle smile. "Our usual groundskeeper is still here," he said as they reached his car. "And he's perfectly capable of maintaining the property." Oakleigh frowned as she tried to think of a response, but her father didn't give her the chance. "Besides, with the synagogue itself now ready for Chanukah, I'm sure you'd like to spend your evenings at home."

Oakleigh silently got into the car, but once her father had started driving them away, she said, "Can't. The Jewish Community Center is putting on a Chanukah party and they're way understaffed. I was going to go there tonight, after everyone else leaves, and get it cleaned and set up just like your synagogue."

Brooks was silent for a few seconds before speaking. "You don't need to go out and work *every* night, dear. Chanukah is a time for celebration and rest."

"Dad, I'm fine." Oakleigh looked out the window as familiar downtown buildings glimmered in the early dawn light. "I'm part golem, remember?"

"Even golems take Shabbos off," Brooks noted. "And besides, you're half human too, and humans need rest."

"I rest on Shabbos, just like Mom." Shabbos night was the only time that Oakleigh and her mother stayed in their human forms and slept. During the rest of the week, Oakleigh was human while it was light out but became a tireless golem after sundown, while her full-golem mother was *always* in her clay body except during Shabbos. "It's not a problem."

Oakleigh glanced back at her father and saw a skeptical expression on his face. "Dad..." she tried again. "Look, it's been a tough year for everyone, right? Not even because of politics and stuff like that, but just in general." Brooks gave a slight nod, as Oakleigh had known he would, since many of his congregants discussed their problems with him. "So I want to use my... powers, I guess... to help them."

"There's nothing wrong with helping people," Brooks said. "But you shouldn't exhaust yourself."

Oakleigh frowned. "I don't get tired when I'm a golem."

"How much time did you spend as a human, earlier today, thinking about the best way to clean the synagogue so you could do it all by yourself in one night?" Brooks asked. "And did all that planning tire you?"

The answers were 'a few hours' and 'yes,' but Oakleigh figured it wouldn't be wise to say that. "Well, the synagogue had to be cleaned, and I couldn't ask anyone to help me. They'd freak out if they saw me when I was, you know. A big clay blob."

Brooks's face quirked up in a slight smile, but he still said, "You could have done it during the afternoon. And perhaps if you told your friends or others in the congregation that it was important to you, they'd have helped."

Oakleigh hesitated. They probably would have, yes, but that missed the point. She was the one who turned into a behemoth creature six nights a week. How could she foist work on other people when she was not only able to do it herself, but was more capable than anyone else thanks to her very nature?

"I got it done, didn't I?" she asked at last. And when Brooks gave a reluctant nod, Oakleigh pressed on. "So I know what I can and can't do, and I'm sure I can help with the JCC too. They really need it, since Chanukah's only two and a half days out, so will you please write me new orders tonight that will let me set the JCC up?"

Brooks was silent for a long moment and Oakleigh tensed, but the rabbi finally nodded. "If it's important to you, of course, dear."

"Thank you, Dad!" Oakleigh grinned. "I'll make it look perfect, I promise."

The rabbi raised one finger off his car's steering wheel as if to call for silence. "But please remember," he added, "that this year, Chanukah both begins and ends during Shabbos. That means you'll be human for two nights of it, and I don't want you to miss them out of exhaustion."

"I won't," Oakleigh promised. "I'll celebrate, and party, and have a great time with everyone else. I promise."

Brooks nodded once more and Oakleigh looked back out the window, already turning over in her head all the work that the JCC needed.

No sooner did the sun set the next night than Oakleigh smiled from her spot hidden in the bushes behind the JCC. She shook as the first beams of moonlight hit her and clay erupted over her entire body, spilling out from beneath her skin and molding over her slim frame until she was twelve feet tall and completely encased in thick earth. She picked up the earthenware tablet her father had inscribed and glanced over the Hebrew characters on its surface once more before cramming it into her gaping mouth. Her jaw rose to seal itself as the tablet's orders stamped themselves in her mind—*Clean the JCC, prepare it for the Chanukah party, don't let anyone see me*—and she rushed to the side door she'd propped open earlier.

But when she got inside, carefully stepping on the tile floor to avoid squeaking and ducking her head so she didn't knock it on the off-white ceiling, she heard footsteps and chatter from around a corner in the hallway. "It's so great you were able to take time off and come down here," said a female voice. Oakleigh vaguely recognized it as belonging to one of the JCC's usual teenaged volunteers, though she couldn't recall the girl's name. "It's been ages since I've seen you!"

"That's why we should make up for lost time." The other voice was a guy's that Oakleigh hadn't heard before, and as he spoke, Oakleigh also heard a couple of popping noises that sounded like someone was opening a couple of bottles. "Brought you your favorite, straight from Boise."

Oakleigh glanced desperately down the hall at a janitor's closet which held the mop and broom she needed, but the third order in her head pressed against her and so she ducked into an unlocked office on her left. She barely fit in the little room and had to huddle with her legs against her chest to avoid knocking into the old folding desk or the other bits of furniture. Her limbs twitched with nervous energy as the urge to obey her first two orders wrestled with the pressure of not disobeying the third, and she tried to tell herself that the speakers would surely leave in just a few minutes.

An hour and a half passed.

"...yeah, that party Stan threw for junior prom was pretty great," said the boy. His voice was languid, like there was no hurry at all to his words, and Oakleigh would have ground her teeth if she'd had any in her golem form. "Hey, you know what? We should see if he and his friends are up for an afterparty once the JCC thing wraps up."

"Ooh, I like the way you think." The girl giggled. "And then after that, maybe you and I could go get a cup of cocoa?"

Oakleigh barely managed to avoid slamming her head down into her clay fists. If she'd been human she could have called out and pretended she was a security guard or something to scare the kids off, but her golem form couldn't talk, and shoving the furniture or otherwise making a racket would risk them investigating and seeing her. All she could do was sit still and think about all the work she had to do. They had to leave soon, she told herself as an old analog clock on the wall marked each second she was wasting. They had to!

Finally, the boy said, "Why don't I drive you home?" Their footsteps neared Oakleigh's office and she glanced through the peephole in the door to see two kids her age, both wearing the yellow volunteer uniforms provided by the JCC, and both holding hands while giving each other excited smiles despite the late hour. But Oakleigh's gaze flashed from their happy faces to the muddy hallway beneath their shoes and she could only twitch with more frustrated energy until they were finally gone.

Oakleigh scrambled to start cleaning the moment she was alone, but the JCC was huge, and she quickly saw that she'd have to prioritize which parts of the building most desperately needed her attention. She almost tripped over her massive feet as she dashed to the big multipurpose room where the main Chanukah party would be held. Though the room was as old and worn as the rest of the building, it was well cared for, and its faded walls were covered with cheerful crayon drawings. Oakleigh distantly remembered being six and making some artwork herself during a summer camp here before she thrust the thought aside. It was time to work.

Sweeping took time. Mopping took more of it. Then Oakleigh turned her attention to several bulging cardboard boxes; they were all full of heavy props and decorations, and someone had piled them up against a wall with locked doors leading to other offices. Oakleigh grabbed the whole pile at once and swiveled to move it but her feet slipped on the floor she'd just mopped. The boxes wobbled and Oakleigh tried to catch them but couldn't stop the last one from toppling over.

The box smacked into one of the locked doors hard enough to rattle it in its frame, and half a second later, a burglar alarm sounded.

Oakleigh fled the JCC and hid in a shadowy alley across the street before a few security guards drove up, but it took them ages to go through the building and conclude it was a false alarm, and even when

Oakleigh scurried back in after they drove off, she could almost feel the clock bearing down on her. The night would end all too soon, and Chanukah was in less than two days, so she *had to* get this done faster, faster, faster...

The sun rose on her just as she was bringing an additional box of heavy decorations from a storage room into the multipurpose area. Even as she shrank back down, the box tore free from her weakening grip to fall against her body, and two paint cans smashed into her before splattering as they knocked her over. And then she was sprawled on the floor, in her human body, dripping with blue paint and staring helplessly at the wall clock telling her she was out of time.

She was still lying there a few minutes later when her father arrived to take her home.

Oakleigh's home had large rooms. It needed them, since she and her mother spent so much of their time as clay humanoids approximately twelve feet tall. But the furnishings in Oakleigh's room were compact, perfectly fitting her smaller frame, and she usually cherished the one night a week when her body stayed human so she could curl up under her bed's thick comforter and rest.

Usually.

But now Oakleigh couldn't keep her frown off her face as she sat up in her bed, stared out her window at the falling snow outside, and wondered how she'd ever get all her work done. Her father had taken her home and she'd gotten herself cleaned off but that hadn't served to cheer her. Nor had her father calling her school to tell them she would be home sick that day. The time off was nice, but she couldn't possibly enjoy it when the JCC still wasn't ready, not to mention all the other things she'd be able to accomplish if she wasn't stuck in the weaker of her two bodies.

· Heavy footsteps sounded by the door and Oakleigh made herself smile so her mother wouldn't think she was sad and worry about her. The older golem entered a second later with a porcelain bowl full of steaming *kartoffelzup,* or potato soup. Her fingers were thicker than Oakleigh's but nimbler too, able to grip the thin bowl without breaking it or spilling a drop of soup, and her clay was more sunbaked and weathered than her daughter's while her eyes had a redder glow to them. "Thanks, Mom," Oakleigh said as she took the bowl. "Just what I needed." And then, too quickly, she added, "I'll finish this and go help—"

Oakleigh's mother shook her head and pointed at the bed until Oakleigh settled back within it. Then she tucked Oakleigh in, brushed her daughter's forehead with an incredibly light touch despite her heavy body, and raised her hands to use sign language. "You need rest," the mute golem said with her fingers. "Stay here. I'll bring you some chocolate in a little bit."

A tiny smile formed on Oakleigh's face at the mention of chocolate, but it only lasted until her mother tidied up a few things and then left. Oakleigh recalled her father describing his rescuing her mother from some catacomb in eastern Europe, and how they'd then spent countless Shabbos days—the only times Oakleigh's mother was human, when she could act for herself and even speak aloud—discovering the things she wanted to do and working out instructions to let her do them instead of standing idle or slavishly obeying commands she disliked. And much of what Oakleigh's mom wanted to do boiled down to 'be useful and help people,' which her father understood, but when Oakleigh wanted the same they insisted she rest.

Why was it so hard for them to get it? She was a golem, she was supposed to work, and with Chanukah coming up and the whole community yearning for a spectacular holiday, she had lots to do to make sure everything went perfectly. Nothing else mattered!

Oakleigh finished her soup and was thinking about trying to sneak out of bed when her door opened again and Rabbi Brooks stepped in. "Feeling a little better?" he asked.

"Yes, Dad," Oakleigh said at once. She pushed her covers back and stretched theatrically. "Lots better, actually. What are you and Mom doing?"

"Getting ready for Shabbos Chanukah tomorrow." Brooks grinned. "I was just about to leave to get the ingredients for the brisket, and your mother is mixing the dough for the *sufganiyot*. You still like those little donuts, don't you?"

Oakleigh nodded. "Sure. And I could get the ingredients for you if you want. The grocery's not that far of a walk and it isn't snowing too badly."

Brooks tilted his head, which Oakleigh knew was his usual prerequisite to asking her probing questions, but there wasn't any way for her to escape it. "Why should you go?" he asked.

"To help you." Oakleigh frowned at her father. "So you don't have to go out in the snow. It's not a problem, really."

"Ah." Brooks smiled. "But if it's good for you to go so I could stay here and rest, why wouldn't it also be good for *me* to go so *you* could stay here and rest?"

Oakleigh grimaced. "You have too much to do. I mean, Chanukah starts tomorrow night."

"Chanukah is a commemoration," intoned Brooks as he sat next to his daughter. "Of our overcoming those who would destroy us. Of the miracle that gave us eight days of light when we only had enough oil for one. And of our survival. It is a joyous time, one marking an end, not a beginning, of our labors, and one where we are called to rest and simply enjoy ourselves with our friends and loved ones. You see that everyone else should put aside their work on Chanukah and celebrate. Why can't you see that you should do so as well?"

"Someone has to do the work to set up the holiday," Oakleigh protested. "I can do it, Dad. I'm strong. And what's even the point of being part golem if I just sit around and don't help people when they need it? Sometimes people need help and it's good to lend a hand, even if it takes some work—"

Brooks smiled. "But you're a person too, Oakleigh."

The two stared at each other before Oakleigh looked away, and Brooks rested a hand on her knee. "Chanukah is for you just as much as it's for any other of our people. And even if it weren't, you wouldn't be happy if your mother and I were exhausting ourselves to the point where we couldn't enjoy the holiday. Isn't that why you rushed to offer me help a few minutes ago?" When Oakleigh nodded, Brooks added, "Then you can see how we, and your friends, and all the other people who care about you wouldn't be happy if you worked yourself to exhaustion and couldn't celebrate."

Oakleigh sighed. "Maybe," she admitted at last. "But there's still lots of work to be done. If the JCC isn't set up, the party can't happen."

"Then the work must be completed," Brooks conceded. "But that does not mean you must do every bit of it on your own."

"How else will it get done? Some of the work, like moving those heavy boxes, I'm not strong enough to do during the day. And if I asked some friends to help and they saw what I look like at night, I'm pretty sure they'd freak out." Oakleigh managed a slight chuckle.

Brooks's eyes twinkled. "Who said they have to see you at night?"

He got up, gave Oakleigh one more warm smile, and trotted out of the room while Oakleigh considered. And after a long moment, a thoughtful look came to her face.

"Okay everybody, let's get started!" Oakleigh smiled at the dozen friends she'd gathered up, some of whom she knew from synagogue and others who were neighbors or classmates. It was a few minutes past mid-afternoon, school had let out for the day, and the group approached the JCC while fresh snow fell around them and filled the air with a bright, cold energy. "And thanks again for helping out!"

"No problem," said Martyn, who had been friends with Oakleigh for close to a decade. He brushed sandy hair away from his dark eyes and added, "You always do so much for us. We're happy to return the favor."

The group split up under Oakleigh's direction and they began, working with the volunteers that the JCC still had on hand to mop, sweep, scrub, and otherwise clean up the old building. They prepared not just the main multipurpose room but all the other spaces that would be needed too, from the playroom for the small children to the rest area for those who got tired and needed to sit down. Oakleigh even led a few of her classmates in shoveling the walk outside.

And when the work was mostly done, the celebratory pizza and sodas had been happily devoured, and everyone else was leaving for the night, Oakleigh went home too and spent a peaceful evening with her family. Neither she nor her parents mentioned any sort of chores as they played cards on the oversized deck Brooks had commissioned and watched a comedy movie Oakleigh had wanted to see. Then Brooks went to bed while the golems stayed awake as usual, with Oakleigh's mother working on one of her many nighttime projects—this one a series of quilts to be donated to a local shelter—and Oakleigh supporting her with some backup stitching.

There were still a few tasks to do at the JCC, of course. Even Oakleigh's group hadn't finished everything in one afternoon. But there truly wasn't much remaining, so Oakleigh didn't take up the special instructions Brooks had written her and return there under cover of darkness until the night was almost over. It took less than half an hour to finish the final tasks: unpacking the last boxes, hauling out a heavy piece of broken equipment from the basement to the dumpster, and pounding down patio pavers that had risen up and might trip people. Then the sun rose, she turned back, and she smiled as she walked home through a light snowstorm and flakes brushed against her freckly face.

Even later, at the service in the synagogue and especially during the party at the JCC, Oakleigh felt an immense lightness and ease filling her. There was no work to do and she could sit back and enjoy the company while eating all the delicacies that had been prepared. The couple she'd overheard the previous night chattered about some romantic restaurant they'd tried out, little children made crayon drawings and taped them to the walls while everyone applauded, Oakleigh's mother sang with the voice she so rarely had an opportunity to use, and Oakleigh—between bites of sweet kugel and sweeter *sufganiyot*—toasted her father and everyone present. "L'chaim!" she cried, beaming as the others giggled at her gleeful enthusiasm. "To life!"

It was a perfect night, she realized as she sat down. It was everything she'd hoped for in a holiday. It was...

It was a time for celebration and rest, just like her father had said. Oakleigh smiled at the thought. And then she leaned back in her chair, relaxed, and let the warmth and joy of the party carry her away.

North Florida is Not the North Pole

By Fran Van Cleave

The rooster crow woke me at what Dad used to call oh dark thirty. That was Dad's funny way of saying it was still dark outside.

I huddled in the warmth of my pajamas under my blanket and quilt, hoping the heater would kick in before I had to get up. My brain always takes a long time to get going before the sun comes up. Especially when there was something I didn't want to think about. If I could just go back to sleep....

Cookie-doo-doo! The rooster was so loud, it was like he was standing right outside my window.

I made a face and pulled the pillow over my head, but it was no use. I'd already remembered it was Christmas Eve.

Taking a deep breath, I promised myself I wasn't going to let it get to me. I threw the covers off and hopped out of bed, shivering as I grabbed my yard clothes and my hoodie. Mom was working day shift today, so she wouldn't know if I turned the heat up. But I'd feel bad about costing us money, and besides, the extra heat would be wasted once I was dressed and in the back yard. By the time I got back, Teddy would be up and building a fire in the fireplace.

Before we moved here, I thought Florida would be all warm and sunny in December. Now I knew there was more than one Florida, and we weren't in the postcard with sunny palm trees. We were in North Florida, home of rednecks and alligators that didn't mind cold winters with no snow.

It's also about as far from the North Pole as you can get in North America.

After pulling on my underwear, jeans, bra, and long-sleeved tee in the bathroom, I brushed my hair, grabbed my winter hoodie and egg basket, and hurried to the back door where I kept my Crocs. I toed them on over the socks I'd worn to bed. I could hear the chickens clucking behind the gate at the top of the porch steps. They did this every day. They think I won't feed them unless they remind me.

Zipping up my hoodie, I threw the door open and stepped out on the porch, its tan paint glinting pink, red, and green with sunrise and the Christmas lights Mom and Teddy put up a week ago. Cookie Monster, his big knobby feet clenched around a porch railing that glittered with frost, let out an ear-splitting crow. Then he hopped down on the porch in front of me and stomped around fluffing his silvery-gray tail-feathers.

I knew the best way to get him back in the yard was to open the gate and throw chicken feed in the grass. But the feed was in the big shed in the back yard.

The other chickens all flew up on top of the gate, clucking wildly.

Like most teens, I'm not a morning person. But wow. As Mom says, they sure knew how to push my buttons.

I stepped forward, waving my arms and shouting, "Boo!"

The chickens squawked and flapped off the gate back into the yard. All except for Cookie Monster, who hopped at me and pecked my leg. He didn't count on me opening the gate and jumping off the steps into the yard.

As I ran for the shed, chickens clucking and hopping around me, I thought for the umpteenth time how great it'd be to have a kitten for a pet. Not one of the feral cats around here. I tried to make friends with one and it bit me.

I wanted a sweet little fuzzy creature who purred and liked cuddles.

Mom said that was a possibility once she got caught up on bills, but vet visits aren't cheap. Even for rescued kitties.

Reaching the shed, I opened the door just wide enough to slip inside, flipped on the light, and grabbed a jar to scoop up chicken feed. I had to chase the chickens out and slam the door before opening the plastic crate that kept bugs out of the feed.

Florida bugs. Don't get me started.

As I scooped out the feed pellets, I noticed the new bag was already half empty. Mom says chickens are pigs with wings. She's not wrong.

I hurried outside, shaking the jar of pellets. The chickens mobbed me, jumping and pecking the jar, all except for Cookie Monster, who'd hopped off the porch into the driveway. I shook the jar harder. Some roosters will let you pick them up, but not this one. If he ran out into the road and got hit by a truck, Mom would be mad. We need Cookie Monster to protect the hens from stray dogs and owls.

Anyway, he suddenly realized I had food. He ran out of the driveway, but instead of going back on the porch, he tried to fly over the wire fence between the carport and the backyard. Mom had clipped his wings when he got big, and he couldn't quite make it.

I dumped nearly all the pellets in the feeder by the chicken coop. Dodging the horde of hungry hens, I hurried back to the porch and into the carport. Cookie Monster hopped up and down, his beady yellow eyes gazing longingly through the wire fence at the feeder.

"C'mon, this way," I said, sprinkling the last of the pellets on the porch. The tiny rattle must not have been loud enough, because he didn't turn, just kept hopping against the fence. With a sigh, I walked up behind him and tried to shoo him up on the porch.

He squawked angrily and flapped his wings so hard, the rush of air made me blink. Then he flew up on my shoulder and launched himself over the fence.

Wincing, I rubbed my shoulder. Good thing I put on my heaviest hoodie. Still, those claws hurt.

I trudged back up on the porch and picked up my basket. Then I went to look for eggs, which was the only part of chicken-keeping I enjoyed.

Between the two nesting boxes and their hiding place under the coop, there were five eggs, more than enough for breakfast for me and Teddy. I placed them carefully in the basket, then got the watering can and went to the garden.

Before we moved here, I thought there was no such thing as a winter garden. To my surprise, some veggies like snap peas, carrots, lettuce, and broccoli love cool weather. They don't like freezing, so we had to cover them up at night, but they seemed pretty happy during the day.

I went to the garden and stopped in shock about two yards away. The garden had a fence around it to keep out the chickens as well as the occasional deer. But now I saw the gate was open and there were lots of holes dug in the garden. At first I thought it must've been the chickens. Then I stepped through the gate and saw the armadillo.

It's a funny-looking creature, with spoon-shaped ears, a long nose, and an armored body with stubby legs, but there was nothing funny about the holes in our garden. It must've been looking for worms or beetles, because they don't really eat veggies. Not much, anyway.

But when they dig with those long claws, they don't need to eat veggies to ruin them. We'd covered the broccoli and peas overnight with old sheets to protect against frost, but some of them still looked to be falling over.

I put down my egg basket and watering can, grabbed a broom from the shed, and ran through the gate after the armadillo. It must've panicked when I started waving the broom. It kind of jumped up in the air, then began galumphing around and around the garden.

Finally it ran out through the gate and I uncovered the sad-looking plants, then tried to fill in the holes before watering. I'd have to come out later and harvest the peas and the broccoli.

Right now I was too hungry. I just wanted breakfast.

Mad at the world and whoever left the gate open, I grabbed my basket and went back in the house to make breakfast. Teddy was up, building a fire in the living room fireplace. I'd left my phone on the kitchen counter, and there was a text from Mom about her plans for dinner when she got home from work. I set down my basket, dropped two slices of bread in the toaster, got out a bowl, and turned on the heat under the pan.

I went out to the living room and asked Teddy what he wanted to drink.

"Hot chocolate!" he said excitedly, pushing his wavy black hair out of his eyes. "See how great the fire looks? And our tree! Aren't the decorations beautiful?"

We'd strung popcorn over the room organizer and hung our Christmas stockings on it. We even put up the little nativity scene with the baby Jesus, which we'd had since I was little.

I agreed that the Christmas tree looked great, and so did the fire. Then I went back to the kitchen, cracked four eggs into a bowl, and melted butter in the hot pan.

If it wasn't for Teddy, I would've told Mom to forget about Christmas this year. But he was only nine. I knew he missed Dad as much as I did, but Teddy still believed in *some* kind of magic at Christmas. Though it was our first Christmas without Dad, Teddy really wanted a traditional holiday.

I whipped the eggs in the bowl, poured them in the hot pan, and went to the fridge to get milk for his hot chocolate.

That's when the power went out. One second the lights were on, and the next, they were off. It was still sunny outside, but kind of gloomy in the kitchen.

"Hey, Val! The Christmas tree lights are out," Teddy said from the living room.

"It's just a power outage," I told him. "We'll make your hot chocolate over the fire."

I sounded calm, but I was annoyed. Talk about a lousy Christmas Eve! I stirred the eggs, telling myself the power would come back on soon. I just wanted to spend the rest of the day on my phone, listening to music.

The stove was electric, so the burner finished cooking the nearly-done eggs in less than a minute. I split them between two plates, pried the toast out of the toaster and put butter on them, and poured a cup of milk into a stainless steel pot. Then I brought one of the plates and the pot into the living room.

"This is great," Teddy said happily as he took the pot. "It's just like camping."

"Did you accidentally leave the garden gate open?" I asked.

"I'm not sure," he said, looking down. "Maybe?"

"Please don't do that again," I said. I wasn't going to tell him about the armadillo, because then he'd get excited and try to find it.

I went back to the kitchen and put cocoa mix in a cup with a spoon and brought that back to him. I told him not to hold the pot over the fire, just leave it in the coals. When I got my own plate, I poured some of Mom's cold coffee in a cup with a little sugar, grabbed my phone, and went back to the living room.

Mom would be really mad if Teddy got burned because I left the room. Sure, it was his job to bring in wood and build the fire, which kept the electric bill down. He managed that just fine. But making hot chocolate on the fire was different. He might not think about his own safety.

But when I got there, he had the pot in the coals like I told him. We both ate our breakfasts, and I told him about Mom's text. I couldn't remember everything she said, so I looked at it again. That's when I noticed that she'd said something about there being a big rain in Tallahassee that froze the power lines.

When Teddy heard that, he said gloomily, "I'll bet that means the power's going to be down for a long time."

I had no idea, but I said the first thing I thought of.

"They'll get extra people to fix it, because of it being Christmas Eve. So probably not that long." That's what I hoped, anyway. The thought of not being able to listen to music or go online all day really depressed me.

Teddy cheered up right away.

"Sure they will! Maybe after dinner, we can drive around and see all the Christmas lights." Carefully picking up the pot, he poured the warm milk in his cup of hot chocolate powder and stirred.

"Okay, why not?" I doubted there'd be many Christmas lights in a town this small. Tallahassee would have a lot more, but it was too far to drive after dinner. Ice on the road made it even worse.

But that probably wasn't the point, not really. Teddy and I had been looking forward to our older brother, Matt, coming home on leave from the Air Force. Matt's leave got canceled at the last minute. Mom had been trying to hide her disappointment, and I knew Teddy wanted to distract himself.

It might even work, for a few minutes anyway. But no amount of Christmas lights would distract us from Dad not being here. Our first Christmas without him. I hated every minute of it.

I finished my breakfast, and just sat there for a minute, drinking cold coffee.

The lights flickered for a second, and my hopes shot up. But then they went dark again and stayed that way.

The spoon clinked in Teddy's cup when he finished his hot chocolate. "Maybe we should go talk to someone about when the power will come back on. I want to listen to Mannheim Steamroller."

"Talk to someone? Like who?" In the six months since we'd moved here, neither of us had made any real friends at school. There were exactly two neighbors within a quarter-mile of us, both of them old people who lived alone, and we'd never spoken to either of them.

"Well, I thought we could ask Mrs. Elliott. She was married to a guy who was an electrical lineman."

I stared at Teddy in confusion. "Who's Mrs. Elliott?"

"Our neighbor. Mom told me a little about her."

"She still married to the electrical guy?"

"No, he died last year."

Thinking it might help, I gulped the coffee. "Then why would we go there?"

"She's bound to know more about electrical blackouts than we do."

I guessed he had a point, but I hated showing up on a strange person's doorstep, let alone asking them questions. Besides, we had plenty of heat from the fire. We could stick it out.

"Please," Teddy said. "I don't want to go by myself."

I sighed. "Okay. Let me get my jacket."

A few minutes later, we were outside, walking across the wet brown grass to the county road we lived on. All the frost had melted into the sandy ground, but the air was humid and there were little puddles everywhere. The only traffic was an old pickup truck rattling by.

Neither of us said anything until we were almost to Mrs. Elliott's house, which had woods on both sides. Then I noticed what looked like hair from a white animal on the road.

"I hope nobody ran over a rabbit," I said.

"Or a cat," said Teddy.

I grimaced. I hadn't thought of that.

Feeling depressed, I walked up her driveway. Christmas lights twisted through her bushes and around her blue and white porch. The lights were dark, just like ours.

Let's just get this over with, I thought.

Teddy knocked on the door. I heard footsteps, and then the door was opened by a thin gray-haired woman in wire-framed glasses, a baggy sweater, stretch pants, and running shoes. She was probably in her fifties.

Ever the chatterbox, Teddy introduced us and asked if she knew anything about when the power might come back on. Mrs. Elliott ran a hand through her short hair.

"I heard some talk on the police band about it. Could be a few hours, they said. No way to really know yet." A gray cat came up and wound around her ankles, and she picked it up.

"Oh," I said, disappointed. "That's a beautiful cat."

"Thank you." She hesitated. "Would you like some cookies?"

"Sure!" said Teddy. "That'd be great."

I liked cookies too, but I wasn't so sure I liked the idea of going in a stranger's dark house.

"Come in and have a seat," she said, opening the door. "There's plenty of light in the living room."

I hesitated, but Teddy didn't, and I saw another cat inside, so of course I went in. She had the smallest Christmas tree I'd ever seen sitting on a side table by the wall. A moment later we were sitting on the sofa, eating chocolate chip cookies. And I had a kitty purring on my lap.

"Mimi's very friendly," said Mrs. Elliott. "But she can't help poking people with her claws when she gets up and down."

I said I didn't mind, that I loved cats. If only rooster claws were that small.

"You didn't happen to lose a cat, did you?"

My stomach tensed. "No, why?"

She frowned. "Unfortunately, one was hit by a car this morning right in front of my house. I would have taken the poor thing to the vet, but she was gone by the time I picked her up. She looked like she's had kittens recently, so there may be some kittens out there somewhere."

Kittens?

Teddy and I exchanged a glance.

"How can we find them?" I asked. Mrs. Elliott pulled off her glasses and rubbed her eyes.

"That's hard to say. They might be out in the woods, or even under any of the houses built on posts."

Teddy cleared his throat. "Doesn't the older man on the other side of us have a hunting dog?"

"You mean Gary Dickerson?" Mrs. Elliott snorted a little. "He has a dog, and he goes hunting, but I don't know if it's a hunting dog."

"We'll ask him," Teddy said, brightening with purpose. "I'll bet he can find them."

I didn't know if it would work, but I couldn't stand the thought of newborn kittens freezing to death.

"Thanks for the cookies," I said, standing slowly to let Mimi jump off my lap. "We'll go ask."

"Okay," said Mrs. Elliott, also standing. "He's kind of a grumpy old Boomer, but he might help you. Let me know how it turns out. Or if you need any help with newborn kittens."

"Great, thanks." It occurred to me that she was actually pretty nice. Why had it taken me so long to say hello to her? "Well, Merry Christmas."

"Merry Christmas, you two. Good luck."

We thanked her again and left. We didn't walk to Mr. Dickerson's house, we ran. Kind of undignified for fifteen-year-old me, but I didn't care. I wanted to find the kittens.

Mr. Dickerson's place was one of the houses on posts, which is popular in Florida. He had a carport with an American flag, a twisty tall pecan tree, and a small front yard littered with a few hundred pecans that'd blown down in the last storm. A couple of cycads, which look like squat palm trees, seemed to be standing guard on either side of his front porch.

There were no Christmas lights anywhere, but the front window showed lights on in his house.

"The power's back on!" I exclaimed. I had to slow down when I reached the walkway to his house, because you can twist an ankle if your foot lands wrong on a big pecan. Ask me how I know.

"How come our house is dark?" Teddy asked. "We should be able to see our living room lights."

"I don't know," I said, puffing for breath as I climbed Mr. Dickerson's porch steps. I was feeling anxious about talking to him, but determined not to look stupid. Or weird. Or both.

I raised my hand to knock on the door, and a dog started barking. I almost didn't knock on the door, but I made myself do it. Knock, knock.

The dog barked even louder.

Footsteps approached, and I heard a man's voice speaking to the dog. Then the door swung open. The gray-bearded man standing in the doorway didn't look very friendly. His silvery hair stuck up as if he'd forgotten to brush it, and he wore an unbuttoned plaid shirt over an old white tee-shirt, jeans, and plaid slippers. The electric light in the room cast shadows on his lined face, which really made him look like he was scowling.

"Yeah?" he said in a gravelly voice.

"Um, hi," I said. "We were wondering if maybe, uh...."

"Could you and your dog help us find some lost kittens?" Teddy said in a small voice.

"I can give you some carrots and sweet potatoes from our garden," I offered. We'd dug up the potatoes in October and still had plenty.

The old man squinted at us. "You're the neighbor kids. The Wilsons. You're mom's a nurse, right?"

I nodded. "And we need help finding some newborn kittens before they freeze to death."

"Well, okay. Guess we could give it a try. C'mon in while I put my boots on. Butch, friends."

Nervously, we stepped inside. The room was pleasantly warm, and the dog stayed where he was, wagging his tail. But wow, he was a really big German Shepherd. I'd seen him before from a distance, but he looked even bigger up close, tan and black and long pink tongue. And lots of big white teeth.

I didn't see a Christmas tree. Maybe he wasn't celebrating this year. Even though I wasn't celebrating either, I was okay with us having a tree. I mean, it made Teddy happy.

Teddy wandered into the kitchen. "Wow, he's got a big turkey on the counter."

"Don't go in there. That's snooping."

About five seconds after he came out of there, Mr. Dickerson reappeared wearing a pair of brown work boots and a light jacket. He snapped a long leash on the dog's collar.

"Let's go, Butch."

The dog sprang up excitedly. Teddy held out his hand to the dog, and the dog sniffed it.

"Nice doggie."

Mr. Dickerson actually smiled at Teddy. "I've got a grandson about your age."

I felt braver now, so I petted the dog's head. His ears were as soft as feathers, and his eyes were friendly.

The old man opened the door, and we all went outside.

"Okay, what's our starting point for tracking down these kittens? Butch needs to pick up the scent, and there's stray cats in this neighborhood."

I told him about what happened to the cat in front of Mrs. Elliott's house, and we went down there. I looked for the cat hair. I didn't see it at first, but then a breeze ruffled the brown leaves beside the road, and I saw a flash of white. I uncovered it for Mr. Dickerson to see.

"Find, Butch."

Butch didn't run ahead, but he was looking around as carefully as if he somehow knew how much I was depending on him. Then he sniffed at the cat hair and the ground around it.

I crossed my fingers and swapped a glance with Teddy. If this didn't work, I wasn't sure what I'd do. Maybe split up and search the neighborhood, including the woods?

The dog sniffed the road and began to trot across the street toward the other big patch of woods that bordered our house. We never went in there because it was a mess of tangled vines and fallen trees, and probably home to snakes. Sure, they sort of hibernated in cold weather, but I bet they'd wake right up if you stepped on them.

My heart sped up at the thought of finding the kittens. I could deal with those creepy woods.

Teddy and I ran after Mr. Dickerson and the dog, who I really hoped was able to follow the cat's movements right back to her nest. As long as nobody stepped on a snake.

Clumps of grass and small bushes crackled under Mr. Dickerson's boots as he approached the woods, the dog pulling at his leash.

Butch plunged into the woods without hesitation.

Wishing I'd put boots on too, I followed.

"We may be getting close here," Mr. Dickerson said. "He's pulling hard."

Almost before he finished speaking, the dog began to bark excitedly.

"Let me see, buddy. Move out of the way."

Oh, God, I thought, *what if the kittens are dead?* But I ran forward anyway.

I stopped short. There, between the big knotty roots of a pecan tree, was a nest of leaves, twigs, and grass. A single pale gray kitten lay curled up like a flower bud beneath a root overhang.

"There you go," said Mr. Dickerson, his voice as jovial as Santa Claus. "Good boy, Butch." He took a treat from his pocket and handed it to the dog, who wagged his tail and gobbled the treat.

"Pretty slick," said Teddy. "I wish I had a dog like that."

Ignoring their talk about how much time it took to train a dog like that, I fell to my knees in the leaves and picked up the half-frozen newborn kitten. The tiny paws were cold, but I could feel its little heart beating.

"It's still alive," I whispered, holding it to my cheek. "Oh, thank you!"

"Got everything you need to take care of that little critter?" Mr. Dickerson asked. "Goat's milk and whatnot?"

"Um, no." I tried not to panic. "Maybe I can mix up some kind of formula in the kitchen."

Mr. Dickerson shrugged. "Mrs. Elliott keeps those little Nubian goats. You might ask her."

"Great idea," Teddy said, reaching out a finger to pet the kitten. "We'll do that."

We all tromped out of the woods. I was too excited to look for snakes. Mom would have to let me keep the kitten! Wouldn't she?

Once we were out of the woods and across from Mrs. Elliott's house, Mr. Dickerson glanced at the kitten and said, "You'll need to warm up the milk, you know. Mrs. Elliott still doesn't have any power, so you can use the kitchen at my place." I must've looked as confused as I felt, because he added, "I'm the only one with a generator."

"Oh," I said lamely. "Sure, that makes sense."

"See you kids in a little bit," he said, and he and the dog went back to their house.

Teddy and I hurried across to Mrs. Elliott's.

"I wish we had a generator," Teddy said.

"At least we've got a fireplace," I said. I was still holding the kitten to my cheek so it could get warm.

Teddy knocked on Mrs. Elliott's door, and she let us in her still-dim living room..

Her eyebrows shot up when she saw the kitten. "Well, well, what a success! I can get this little creature some goat's milk, but...."

"Mr. Dickerson already said we could warm up the milk on his stove."

"He would have a generator, wouldn't he?" Mrs. Elliott rolled her eyes. "Still, that's nice of him."

She went to the kitchen and came back with a Pyrex bowl with milk, an eyedropper, and a small terrycloth towel, which she wrapped around the kitten. "You'll probably need to feed her every two hours. Don't worry about her eyes not opening. That won't happen until ten days after they're born."

"Will you come with us?" I asked, cuddling the little bundle. "I can use some more tips, and it's not like I can sign on to Instagram or anything." When she hesitated, I added, "Unless you're getting ready for Christmas Eve. In that case, never mind."

Mrs. Elliott's smile looked a bit wobbly. "No, I'll be glad to come with you."

So we all went over to Mr. Dickerson's. On the way, Teddy ran back in our house to bag up some of the sweet potatoes from our garden.

At Mr. Dickerson's, Butch greeted us like we were old friends, but he had to be introduced to Mrs. Elliott. Mr. Dickerson and Mrs. Elliott eyed each other warily but seemed friendly enough as we went into the kitchen. To my surprise, the place was neat and clean and the air smelled of cooking turkey.

"You're making Christmas dinner?" Mrs. Elliott said, sounding as surprised as I was.

"I shot this turkey yesterday, but then I found out my son and his family aren't coming." Mr. Dickerson shrugged. "They got held up by a little medical emergency, so I guess me and Butch will eat the turkey."

"You can have these with it." Teddy held up the bag of potatoes.

"Sure," said Mr. Dickerson, pouring the goat's milk in a saucepan and turning on the burner. Even I could see he wasn't in a great mood.

Teddy looked around at everyone. "Why don't we all have Christmas dinner together, when my mom comes home?"

I looked up from the kitten, horrified. "You don't invite yourself to Christmas dinner!"

"I wasn't, not exactly. We could bring the mashed potatoes Mom made and could heat them up, and the blueberry pie, too. We could even bring the ham."

I almost said no, but then realized it wasn't a terrible idea. Mom worked such long hours, it was really hard for her to cook much on holidays. But how would she feel about this?

The old man laughed.

"There's plenty of turkey. I don't mind as long as you kids help dish it out. I've got cornbread, too."

"You'll need gravy," said Mrs. Elliott, testing the warmth of the milk and filling up the dropper. "That's easy to make if you've got flour. And you'll need to pop the sweet potatoes in the oven right away if you want them done in time." It kind of seemed like she liked the idea of this dinner.

She handed me the dropper, and I put it to the kitten's mouth. At first it seemed not to know what to do, but then it tasted the milk. It let out the tiniest squeak and began sucking the dropper.

"Success," said Mrs. Elliott, clearly pleased. "Now, how would your mom feel about eating dinner with a bunch of strangers?"

I smiled back at her and refilled the dropper.

"You guys aren't really strangers. I mean, you're our neighbors. I'll text her and ask." Probably the real challenge would be the kitten.

"Oh, she'll be happy," Teddy said, petting the dog, who'd followed us into the kitchen. "She's always telling us about how Christmas is supposed to be about togetherness."

Mom was surprised when I texted her, but she was fine with it.

As we sat down to dinner, which was in our house since the power came back on, a knock sounded on the door. I got up to answer it. The kitten had fallen asleep in my hoodie pocket, and I had a big smile on my face. Mr. Dickerson had been telling dad jokes, and he was pretty funny.

My older brother Matt was standing on the doorstep. "Hey, Val. Merry Christmas."

"Oh, my God! You made it!"

"I tried calling you earlier to tell you my leave was on again, but calls weren't going through due to the power outage." He gave me a big hug. "Looks like everything's okay now, though."

"More than okay," I told him. "It's pretty good, actually."

I looked at the nativity scene on our room organizer.

I didn't know if this was a miracle, but it sure seemed like one to me. I will always miss my dad, but I knew he'd want us to have a good Christmas.

Christmas on Mars

By Richard Cartwright

"How about this one, Pa? Does it have the magic?" The fir looked like something from a Christmas card—tall, and green with a light dusting of snow.

Pa walked over from Thunderbolt, boots crunching in the snow. He eyed the tree, giving it the same look that told me he was measuring if it would fit in the living room. Pa nodded.

"It'll do nicely." Smiling, he handed me the saw. "You cut it, son."

I brushed the snow away from the base and started cutting, face in the bottom branches. The pine scent mixed with the biting cold air as I cut just like Pa had taught me.

Trumpets from the theme of an old Twentieth Century movie that my parents faithfully watched every May fourth blared. I blinked out of December in Montana to staring at the rock ceiling of my room.

"Hank, time to get up, or we'll miss the shuttle."

I fumbled for my phone and snoozed the alarm. Before I could snuggle back into the blankets they were snatched out of my hands. Cold air raised goosebumps on my bare legs.

"Rise and shine, champ! Your mom and Shappa's making breakfast burritos. We need to get the stock squared away since we'll be gone most of the day. We'll eat on the shuttle."

"I'm awake. I'm awake," I muttered around a yawn.

"Sure you are. Get dressed."

I pulled on my thermal underwear, pants, pullover, and boots. Pa shoved a cup of coffee in my hands after I zipped up my jacket. I took the lid off and sniffed, then sipped. My brain started firing.

"Thanks, Pa."

We cycled out of the lock that kept our underground home warm and pressured to what Ma called, "Denver springtime." Icy air knifed my lungs until I adjusted the preheater on my mask. I skipped the supplemental oxygen and looked at the rising sun.

"I'll never get used to morning skies going from blue into caramel," Pa said over his mask's external speakers.

We stood on the porch of our home, built into a crater wall near Gusev Crater, close to where the Spirit Rover made its last stop. The surrounding hills were a mix of red Martian rock and the deep green lichen that was clearing the Martian soil of the salts that would kill even adapted Earth plants. The bison loved it. I followed Pa to the agrodomes and chores.

We got the cows milked, horses and orphaned calves fed along with the chickens. My best friend and blood brother Billy helped speed things along even though it wasn't his day for barn duty. I handed him the basket full of eggs I'd collected for his stepmother Shappa, the ranch cook. He gave me another cup of coffee in return.

"Drink up." He wrinkled his nose. "You have just enough time to get a shower before the shuttle bus touches down."

The shuttle bus lifted from the ranch landing pad. Passing over the hill just beyond the domes of the Triple T, I spied the hill that remined me so much of Christmas Tree Hill back at the ranch my namesake founded after the Civil War in Montana, the Tall T. *Just no trees and no magic.*

Pa always told the story at Christmas that Santa Claus himself led Big Hank to Christmas Tree Hill to find the first tree he erected in the rough cabin that served as the first bunkhouse. Supposely, the right tree would always glow for Hank and provide happiness for those who shared it.

That first winter nearly killed Big Hank and the men who followed him out of the war-ravaged South to a new start in the wilds of Montana. The story goes that he and his men erected the tree in the rough cabin that served as the first bunkhouse. They decorated it with shiny bits of tin cans, whittled animals and bits of scrimshaw carved from elk antlers. They sang Christmas carols around it after a Christmas dinner of beans and cornbread. Big Hank's diary entry credited that Christmas as raising spirits enough to get him and his hands through that brutal winter.

Of course, the diary also said that a plump white bearded mountain man with a red cap showed Big Hank where a stand of fir trees was. *I guess tales get taller in over three hundred years of telling.* I settled down for a nap.

An hour later, I awoke and looked out the window at a bison herd munching on the plains of mutated lichen below us. The green stretched to the horizon. Managing the free-range buffalo was the main reason Pa packed us up to emigrate to Mars in the first place.

According to my Martian history teacher, the Martian Terraforming company selected bison for adaptation to Mars because of their tolerance to cold and ability to thrive on meager fodder. Thanks to an open gate between agrodomes, the scientists, including Ma, who ran the program, learned bison loved the genetically modified lichen whose roots absorbed and concentrated the percolates that doomed any attempt to grow Earth plants in Martian soil.

The scientists also discovered a fact any farmer or rancher grows up knowing. Bovines are self-propelled fertilizer generators. The lichen flourished around the cow patties almost as much as the occasional radiation storm that overwhelmed the artificial electromagnetic shield that was still a work in progress.

The herds could weather the occasional radiation storm, but the animals suffered. The eggheads decided the bison needed to be managed. Robots have always been the pioneers of Martian exploration and development. The engineers all thought that humaniform robots would make excellent cowboys.

I remembered Pa and me howling with laughter at the video Ma sent us from Musk City of the early attempts to use robots to manage a small herd. She'd been on her second sabbatical to Mars, working on adapting bison to Martian conditions.

"I wonder if robots are eligible for Darwin Awards?" Pa managed to get out between guffaws as a white and black colored automaton bounced off the curved dome after getting between a cow and her calf. The lower Martian gravity let the buffaloes get a lot more loft than Yellowstone bison could manage with stupid tourists.

After the herd reduced the twelfth robot to scrap, even the engineers had to admit that some things can't be automated. At least where buffalo were concerned.

The plane jolted, knocking me out of my reverie and causing Ma to squeak. She hated flying and started every trip with either a sleep mask or an immersive VR headset over her eyes. I felt bad for her, but I always got the window seat.

I could just see the outskirts of Musk City approaching from the front part of the thick porthole. Today marked the opening of the Christmas Market. Ma, who had done a fellowship in Germany before she met Pa, said that it was part fair, part shops, and lots of food. Rural Montana had nothing like it.

"I'll meet up with you two at lunch." Ma stuffed her sleep mask into her laptop bag as she got up. The other passengers stayed in their seats until she exited the shuttle. I looked over at Pa.

"They're just being neighborly. Everyone knows Jenny hates flying and are kind enough to let her get off first."

We were the last to descend the jet way. The underground terminal that serviced the air shuttles looked like it had doubled in size since the last time I was here.

Pa passed the taxi stand and joined the crowd of pedestrians on the right side of the tunnel.

"Let's walk; I want to stretch my legs."

I jogged to catch up. I loved Pa, but he was always forgetting that a leisurely walk for his thirty-six-inch legs set a brisk pace for my far shorter stride.

The changes all around me from the last time I was here soon pushed my straining legs out of my mind. The number of storefronts and doorways dotting the tunnel wall along the sidewalk had doubled. A woman in paint-splattered coveralls was outlining "Ted Jones, Attorney at Law" in gold paint on one plate-glass window.

Musk City was growing like the Old West boomtowns I'd read about. When we first emigrated from Montana, not quite a year ago, the town consisted of two dozen interconnected tough clear plastic domes where soil was conditioned by the lichens, and then developed to raise Earth plants and animals to feed the growing colony.

The domes were necessary to protect the terraformed soil from contamination by the perchlorate-laden Martian dust. The hope was that eventually the Earth plants could adapt to the Martian climate.

People lived in a hodgepodge of repurposed first-wave Starship landers buried under the soil and purpose-built underground habitats, all interconnected by tunnels to each other and the domes.

According to my teacher, Mr. Burke, the real game changer was the discovery that the electromagnetic field first developed to shield the Martian settlements could be scaled to protect the entire planet.

The successful deployment of the constellation of emitter satellites, powersats, and control nodes meant we didn't have to wait for a far thicker atmosphere and the creation of an ozone layer to expand settlements. Something that all the scientists initially said would take at least three hundred Earth years to accomplish.

The atmosphere project itself was progressing far faster than the most optimistic predictions. The air was already breathable, if thin and cold. The Tall T on Earth had been about six thousand feet above sea level. Ma had scolded Pa about overdoing when we first started working in the Martian normal, equivalent to about 11,000 feet on Earth.

We were lucky. Some of my friends that came over with us on the Buzz Aldrin cycler hailed from South Texas and suffered from bouts of altitude sickness till they acclimated.

A blinking sign caught my attention, spelling out "Market Dome" in flashing green letters next to an arrow pointing to a branch in the sidewalk sloping up. A steady stream of people, many pushing strollers or wearing slings with babies like Indian papooses, split off from the main sidewalk. Pa and I followed them up the ramp, breaking out into the light.

Moist air laden with earthy smells, overlaid by the faint aroma of pine, tickled my nose. The people exiting behind us nudged us to the rail across from the dome entrance.

The other side of the dome stretched about two football fields away. Four deep green circles dominated the space at ground level. The larger gaps between the circles held what looked like raised planting beds containing small sapling-sized trees.

A placard on the rail explained that the deep green areas were the footprints of the original plastic fabric domes. The new dome had been blown like a soap bubble over the old domes. The saplings were fruit and nut trees, some already bearing fruit.

"I wonder if there're any apples for sale?" Pa mused.

"Pa, I thought we were here to find a Christmas tree?"

"Among other things. Things that fit in our budget."

"Budget" was a word that came up a lot around the table at mealtimes after we got to Mars. Usually with Pa or Ma saying, "It's not in the budget this year. Maybe next."

Building a ranch from scratch is expensive. Things we'd make or repair in the shop, or run off a print of either weren't easy, or even possible on

Mars. The Tall T had nearly two hundred and fifty years of accumulated tools, equipment, tack, and infrastructure. The Triple T had the tack we brought. Everything else had to be bought.

Something as simple as a hammer that had had the wooden handle replaced fifty times had to be bought new on Mars. Making things out of wood was right out. The only wood on Mars consisted of carefully nurtured trees.

I had read that the scientists were trying to adapt pine and other cold-weather species to grow unprotected on the surface. The Martian outdoors was like being at the tree line of tall mountains. Trees can't thrive in thin air and brutal cold. The air was going to have to get thicker before we'd see woods like Montana on our Martian spread.

Much less Christmas trees. Which is why we were looking to purchase a holiday tree for the first time in my life. Even Pa was a little uncertain about buying a tree instead of just riding up to the ranch Christmas grove Thanksgiving Day. I overheard him mutter, "I wonder if any of them will glow?" more than a few times when the topic came up.

Christmas music started up, drawing my eye toward the sound. I realized that was where the pine smell was coming from as well. Pa glanced at his comm unit.

"0900 hours, right on the dot. Your mother was going to take an early lunch and meet us around 1030. We can take our time and see what the regular merchants have on offer."

The first stalls we encountered were produce vendors. Stalls with strawberries, blackberries, blueberries, and even pineapples for sale were common, as were potatoes, carrots, onions and green beans. Lots of peanuts.

"We need to come back and put in an order for the ranch. Those are some good prices. Shappa has been telling me she's tired of using freeze-dried veggies."

About halfway to the section where the holiday market began, Pa found some apples. His face fell when he looked at the price. Turning away, I could hear him grumble, "I could get a ten-pound bag on Earth for the price of one of those."

It wasn't just the apples. Even I knew that seven gold dollars for an orange the size of my fist was a lot of money. The only cherries on offer were dried with a placard stating, "imported from Washington state, Earth."

"Are there any fresh cherries?" I asked. The vendor chuckled.

"Check back in another three or four Earth years. Cherry trees take a long time to grow from seeds."

The produce stalls gave way to craftsmen. I pointed out a booth with belts, and even shoes on display to Pa.

"I didn't expect to see anyone working leather on Mars." The man laughed at Pa's words.

"My day job is as an agronomist. My dad was a cobbler. He taught me the trade growing up. I was able to work my way through school. When he died, I inherited all his tools, and the estate shipped them all here."

"This is all imported leather?"

"Nah. The tools gathered dust until the buffalo carcasses started coming in. I offered to use my off time to skin them in exchange for keeping the hides. And here we are," he said, waving at his stock. He stuck out his hand. "Antonio Sylverstri."

"Trent Thornton. This is my son, Hank."

Antonio released Pa's hand and took mine. "Good to meet both of you." He looked back at Pa.

"You're married to Jenny Thornton? One of the ranchers the colony brought in?"

"Correct on both counts."

"We need to talk about what you're doing with buffalo hides."

While Pa talked business with Mr. Sylverstri, I looked at his table. Pieces of leather in the shapes of stars, bells and Christmas trees caught my eye. Some were dyed green, gold and red. Others were brown. There were holes poked in the tops. And no prices.

I waited for a lull in the conversation. "Excuse me, Mr. Sylverstri, what are these?"

"My contribution to the Christmas Market. I made them out of scrap pieces of leather. There's a guy selling decorations as part of the tree sales that has them on his table. Tell him Antonio sent you. He'll give you a discount."

Pa's comm sounded off to the opening bars of a song that he and Ma get all mushy over.

"Jenny? Good. Okay, we're on our way." He put away his comm. "Let's get a move on, Hank. Your mother's seminar was postponed, so she has the rest of the day off. She's at the tree store right now."

He turned to Antonio. "Here's my comm code. Let's talk more. We need someone who can repair and replace tack, if you're willing to learn the skills. I figure we can keep you in bison hides."

"Sounds good, Trent. I'll look for your call."

We didn't stop at any more booths, although there were a lot of interesting ones. The pine scent got stronger and was joined by the aromas of fresh baked goods, vanilla and other scents as Pa strode down the causeway.

He slowed at an arch made of two candy canes. A sign hung from the crooks. Green and red letters spelled out "Musk City Christmas Fair."

Ma waved at us from a line of Christmas trees. She had that neutral look that usually meant "the roast burned" or "I have to go on a trip." Nothing good came of that look.

Pa stopped so fast I nearly ran into him. "Uh oh," he murmured. He strode to Ma and gave her a hug and a kiss.

"The tree prices..." she whispered almost too softly for me to hear. "I don't think they're in the budget."

I inspected some of the price tags. And blinked. I had seen what our tickets to go from Earth to Mars cost. The smaller trees—ones we'd leave to grow another five years or so at home—were about half of what my fare to emigrate was. A couple of the bigger trees were twice that.

"At least none of the trees glow." Pa sighed. Ma rolled her eyes but smiled.

"Perhaps you haven't found the right trees."

A group of people clustered around a section of clearly artificial trees toward the back. Those trees were a little taller than me and green. A few were shiny silver. I had seen such in movies. I remembered how fake they looked.

The shiny trees were the least expensive of the lot.

"It's 100% Martian-made. The branches are made of an iron alloy. The leaves are aluminum. We have some painted green that don't cost much more."

A guy a little older than me in an elf suit right out of "Rudolph the Red-Nosed Reindeer," Spock ears and all, had come up while I was examining the branches. I understood now why the strips attached to the metal branches felt just like aluminum foil. Almost eight feet tall, the price was five percent of the cost of one of the smaller live trees. The green aluminum trees were just ten dollars more.

"What are you looking at, son?"

The elf answered Pa, "One hundred percent Mars made Christmas Trees sir. We stock them because we know just how expensive it is to get a live tree, especially since we have to ship them with the root ball. Anything we don't sell, the terraforming company buys for research. My father and mother are part of the group trying to adapt Earth trees to Mars."

"I can't imagine a tree that isn't living and..."

Ma cut him off.

"Trent, an artificial tree wouldn't be bad. That's what I had in my apartment after I moved from home. It would give us more to buy ornaments with."

Ma grew up in the city. Pa liked to say that, "the experience didn't do her any permanent harm." She'd said her folks bought a tree every year at a holiday market. That, plus her time in Germany, was why she'd been so excited about the announcement of the Christmas Market in Musk City.

"We can get lights and some more tree decorations," she'd said last night at dinner. We'd only been able to squeeze a few ornaments, mainly the ones that Ma and Pa had bought since they got married and after I was born, into the family weight allowance. "Plus Christmas Markets are full of surprises."

I started to say something about the leather ornaments we saw when Pa spoke.

"Let's talk about it over lunch." He turned to the guy in the elf suit. "How late are you open?"

"Forty-five minutes before the last shuttle departure... tonight that will be 1800 hours." A shout from behind him caused him to turn.

"Hector, I need your help with the seedlings." A woman dressed as Mrs. Claus was operating a forklift carrying a pallet of green twigs that reminded me of the ones we planted every year we harvested a tree on the ranch.

The boy rolled his eyes. "I can't get it through her head that nobody is taking the seedlings." He paled when he realized he'd said that out loud. He raised his voice to a conversational level. "If you'd excuse me, I need to go help my mother." He rushed away.

Ma led us to a food court a few minutes from the Christmas trees. Booths selling everything from sub sandwiches to sushi formed a semicircle around a group of metal folding tables and seats.

I was eyeing a banner proclaiming "Real Southern BBQ" skeptically, when Ma grabbed my shoulder to steer me to an operation that took up nearly a third of the semicircle. The area had a roped-off section festooned with red and green bunting and German flags enclosing its own seating arrangement. A banner with the words "Erika's Edelweiss Haus" had pride of place over the entrance to the seating.

"Trish at work raved about their food. Let's try it."

"Since it's that or 'Real Southern BBQ' that's smoke had to have come out of a bottle, let's go with Trish's suggestion." Pa replied to Ma dryly.

We were lucky we arrived when we did. The place filled up just after we got seated. There were a dozen people in line by the time the server got back to us with menus.

"She said to get here early to beat the lunch rush. I see why now."

Erica's wasn't like a food cart where you waited on your order and moved to the common seating. This place had actual human waiters and waitresses that were all young and looked related.

Looking over the menu, I didn't recognize any of the dishes. There was a kiddie menu. I was twelve years out and wasn't about to eat stuff I could get anywhere. Well, anywhere on Earth. Instead of hot dogs and hamburgers, there were links and meat patties with potato wraps rather than buns.

Pork schnitzel, Jager schnitzel. Something called "der Bison Rouladen" caught my eye, primarily because it had "limited availability, ask for price" beside it.

"What's jager schnitzel? And spaetzle?"

"Jager schnitzel is a fried meat cutlet, probably pork here, that is covered with mushroom gravy. Spaetzle is a kind of pasta, like egg noodles. I'm going to order it. I think you'd like it." Ma beamed.

"I think that's what I am going to get, too." Pa flicked his fingers on the smart sheet, scrolling down. "They have beer. I wonder if Kartoffelbier is a local brand?"

Ma was about to say something when our waitress came up. All the girls had dresses with poofy shoulders that Ma had mentioned were traditional. Ours had a name tag with "Petra" on it. "Are you ready to order? She had a slight accent that sounded like Germans on video.

"Three Jager schnitzels with spaetzle." Pa ordered for us.

"Drinks?" Ma ordered tea. I ordered soda.

"Tell me about the Kartoffelbier?"

"Yes sir. Vater makes it, I'm told that it tastes like a pale lager. Would you like one?"

"Yes, please. If you don't mind my asking, I'm a rancher. I know how difficult it is to get grain, since most of what's grown is going to the bison project. The price for the Kartoffelbier is very reasonable."

"Oh, he doesn't use grain. Vater brews it with potatoes. I'll have your orders right out." She rushed away before Pa could say anything.

Pa's mouth hung open for a second. Then he shook his head and chuckled. "You can make vodka out of potatoes. Why not beer?"

We were just getting up to leave when a big man in a white jacket came out and strode toward the table.

"Excuse me. My Petra tells me that you're a rancher?" He had a slightly stronger accent than our waitress.

"Yes, Trent Thornton." Pa and the man shook hands.

"Niklas Weber; my wife and I cook when we aren't working in the geology division of the terraforming company."

Pa laughed.

"Seems like everyone we've met on Mars has a side gig."

"The colony is too big not to have things like restaurants and merchants. But not quite big enough to allow people to emigrate strictly to run those businesses. Erika and I are getting ready to retire. We were in the second wave. Our children were born here. We have no ties to Earth anymore."

"So, you're staying?" Ma interjected.

"Ja, cooking is our hobby. And one we are turning into our 'second act,' if you will." He turned to Pa. "I have to get back to the kitchen, but I would like to swap contact information with you to discuss supplying buffalo meat. My contact in the agro domes tells me that the program that sourced slaughtered animals for consumption is being discontinued in favor of the ranchers' handling working with the animals in the field."

"Sure thing." They touched comms and both beeped.

"Thank you. I will contact you this evening." The chef turned away.

On the way back to the Christmas trees, Pa filled Ma in on our meeting with Mr. Anthony.

'You've been busy," Ma teased.

"Just trying to fit in," Pa replied, grinning. His face got serious. "The stipend that the colony is paying to manage the herds is nice. But people..." waving at the food court, "need to eat. The guys doing the space mining would probably like to come home to an occasional steak rather than reconstituted freeze-dried all the time."

"And we supply that need." Ma smiled.

"We're going to have to cull the herds both to strengthen them and keep the size manageable enough to get them under cover if the EM shield hiccups. Losing a percentage to radiation sickness is shortsighted as well as cruel. Their growth is going to be a function of building sheltered feedlots. No reason we can't have multiple income streams that would speed up construction and development."

"Not to mention increasing the budget." Ma sighed. "I think compromising on the green artificial tree is our only genuine option."

Pa looked like he'd stepped in a cow patty. Then he looked sad.

"Oh, I agree; I'm just going to miss the smell of pine. The idea of no tree from the Hill just takes the magic out of Christmas for me."

"Your check, sir?" Petra handed him a tablet.

I think Pa missed the twinkle in Ma's eyes while he was thumbing the bill.

Hector was glad to see us come back. He demonstrated how to disassemble and reassemble the tree. Ma and Pa sent me to look at the ornaments that they were selling for Mr. Anthony while they took our tree apart.

I had selected several shapes and colors for the folks to look at when Hector cleared his throat. "Do you think your parents will take a sapling or two? They're leftovers from the latest planting project. Mother's making me offer one for every sale." He shook his head. "The people buying real trees don't want to mess with a stick with tiny branches. The ones buying the artificial trees mostly live in tight quarters, and if they're going to have a plant, it's going to be something bushy and colorful."

"We have quite a bit of room. But our agro dome ceilings aren't real high. I don't think they'd be big enough to grow these in."

"They are designed to survive Mars' normal conditions. They just need a few months in dome conditions to establish themselves."

I thought about everything I had seen today and Pa talking about "multiple income streams."

"How many can we take?"

Mrs. Claus came out of the back. She had a box of fourteen seedlings in her hands. She was making a beeline to Ma.

"My mother's coming. Let me ask her. Mom. These folks want to take as many seedlings as we can give them."

She didn't answer her son, instead speaking to Ma. "Here's your order, Jenny. The seeds took to the manipulation and forced growth better than I expected. So you want some more seedlings as well?"

"They...they glow," Pa whispered.

Fourteen potted pine seedlings made the living area smell almost like Christmases past, although the holographic fireplace didn't cast the heat or smell like the real one in Montana. We still sat in front of it, sipping eggnog and nibbling on leftover cookies. The Christmas Eve party with the hands had broken up about half an hour ago with the last carol, "Silent Night," and it was just us.

The tree looked good decorated with the ornaments from Montana interspersed with the leather stars, bells and Christmas tree cutouts. The lights, which had started out life as trail markers for excavation sites, twinkled.

Pa had taken strands designed for "caution," "go," and "danger," and mixed the colors, so now they were draped around the tree, even the little ones, blinking green, yellow, and red.

"The hands needed that. Some of them had told me how homesick they were. I think the smells of home and knowing we have a little bit of the Tall T here are going to make a big difference for morale," Pa mused.

Over dinner, Ma had told the story of how she had gathered a bunch of seeds from the trees at the Tall T Christmas grove and persuaded Mrs. Claus, or Doctor Minerva Potter, who headed up the plant genetics section of the terraforming company when she wasn't dressing like Santa's wife, to tinker with the seeds and grow them as a surprise for Pa and me.

Pa claimed they glowed like the chosen Christmas tree did on Earth. I nodded but wondered if hallucinations indicated an incomplete adaptation to the thinner air.

After I told Ma and Pa my idea, they not only agreed to take an additional dozen with us but worked out a deal with Doctor Potter to take any leftovers after the fair ended.

"Hank, you have a lot of work ahead of you. I applaud your initiative, but I don't expect you to slack on your chores."

"I won't, Pa, Billy is going to help me with the planting and transplanting."

"I'm surprised that nobody thought about it before now," Pa mused.

"Trent, this is really the first year that Earth trees of any kind would have a chance of surviving in Martian conditions. Even so, they will grow slower than they would on Earth."

"But they should be ready to sell in five or six Earth years, according to Hector. Eventually, the ranch will have its own Christmas tree grove," I replied.

"How about this one, Dad?"

A ten-year-old girl speaking with the tone of her grandmother cut in before I could reply. "No, silly. That's one of the fourteen. It's too big, anyway."

I chuckled, remembering that long-ago Christmas. Those seedlings had grown out to rival a Christmas-card tree.

It had taken a lot of spare time, both mine and Bill's, but by the time we had to pass the project on to the younger kids on the ranch, we had built enough soil to cover the hill overlooking the ranch in trees from the first fourteen to new saplings. It might have been selfish, but we never sold any tree descended from the Tall T stock.

Between us and some other ranches and farms, Mars hadn't imported Christmas trees for over twenty-five Earth years. People still bought trees every year. And planted them after Epiphany with the blessings of the terraformers.

Hank Junior moved to another tree. I eyed it to make sure it would fit. And that it glowed.

"It'll do nicely."

Dad's Cookie Jar

By Sophie G. Michaels

"What do you think?" Mícé whispered, half afraid someone important might overhear them. "Could she be right?"

"There's no way," Drù replied. "He has to be real."

"But she's always right."

"Sure, in class. But this isn't school."

"She's not the only one saying it, though. I just didn't believe any of it till she said so."

Drù didn't want to admit it, but Lana's announcement this morning worried him too. Lana was much smarter than everyone else in class. She *always* had an answer ready when their teachers asked a question, and she was *never* wrong. Even when she was talking about something that wasn't about school.

But now she said that Santa couldn't be real.

He *had* to prove her wrong.

Because if she wasn't, then his parents and everyone he knew was lying to him. And all those stories he loved were nothing but stories.

Even his favorite, the one about his cookie jar.

"She has to have been wrong about something before," he insisted. "Even Mom and Dad are wrong sometimes."

"Not that I know of."

Mícé looked as unhappy about it as he was.

"Well, she's wrong about this," Drù insisted. "We just have to figure out how to prove it."

This week, Aunt Mixele was the after-school parent. Drù really liked those weeks, especially around the holidays. They were usually even better than when Daddy or Mama had the job. Daddy was fun and Mama always had a special surprise, but Aunt Mixele always had special treats for the after-school snacks. And of course, she was always super nice.

The two boys lagged behind their classmates like usual, though they managed not to get distracted by the playground, where all the babies and creche children were playing or getting some air with their parents or caretakers. The pool would have been more distracting if the first real cold front of the season hadn't made Drù glad he was wearing a light jacket today.

He even managed to avoid the temptation of the little forest between the pool and community garden, until he caught a glimpse of white in the spaces between the last few pines and scrub palms of the forest.

He left the path and darted off after Mícé.

The white picket fence surrounding the garden had been built to keep out the automower and community pets, not little boys. Drù tossed his backpack over the fence. Then he stuck his right foot in between two of the pickets and used the board that supported them to push himself up. He swung his left leg over the fence and followed it over, dropping onto the soft mulch on the other side. Then he went to the gate to let Mícé in, because he was stockier and had more trouble getting over the fence.

Drù usually enjoyed looking at the pumpkins or whatever else was growing, especially when it was something like tomatoes or strawberries that he could eat right there. Pumpkins were like watermelon. They didn't look like food at all until they were cut open. Pumpkins didn't even really look like food then. He wasn't sure what they looked like, but the dried and twisted vines attached to them looked like they could creep right out of the garden.

But today, all he could think about was Lana's surprising announcement. How could he and Mícé prove that Santa was real, when she was so sure he wasn't?

And what if Lana was right? All his life, everyone he knew told him stories about Santa. Even Mama told him Santa stories, though hers were ones like *The Night Before Christmas* that came in books instead of ones about the family.

Once, last year, he'd asked Daddy why that was. Daddy had told him it was because she had married into the family instead of being born into it the way they had.

That had surprised Drù. Mama and Daddy had been together as long as he'd known them. He'd just assumed they'd always been married.

Drù was about to ask Mícé if his family had any special presents from Santa or just the ones he brought everyone on Christmas Eve night when Mícé turned from where he was comparing two of the bigger pumpkins.

"I know how we can prove Santa's real!" he yelled.

"Yeah?" Drù yelled back, running over. "How?"

"We stay up late on Christmas Eve and watch for Santa!" Mícé exclaimed. "If we see him, we know he's real!"

"Don't you mean Saint Nick's Eve?" Drù asked, confused.

That was when Santa always came to pick up all the presents they'd gotten for poor families. He really liked it when Mama and Daddy let him pick out the toys that went under the tree the first time around.

Santa always took those presents away in the middle of the night and helped himself to some of whatever baked goods had been put out.

Drù vaguely remembered one year, two or three years ago, when Mama was sick all the time and they'd put out store cookies instead of homemade.

Santa hadn't touched the store cookies.

"What's that?" Mícé asked.

"You don't know about Saint Nick's Eve?" Drù asked. "It's the best! Mama and Daddy make a bunch of Christmas food and my cousins come over and we finish decorating the tree and everything and— "

"I wanna come!" Mícé begged. "When is it?"

"I don't know."

Drù racked his brain.

"It's just after Thanksgiving, but long enough after that it's in December. I think. I can ask Mama."

Drù had progressed from telling Mícé all about Saint Nick's Eve and was telling him about Saint Nick's Day when the fence post closest to the boys suddenly chimed.

The boys jumped.

"Drù Sabret!" Aunt Mixele's voice came over the speaker. "You and your friend Mícé were supposed to come here straight from school. If you don't hurry, there won't be any snacks left."

Oh no!

"We're on our way!" both boys exclaimed.

"Don't forget your backpacks," Aunt Mixele added. "And your jackets, if you took them off."

Drù ran over to where he'd dropped his backpack, while Mícé picked his up and ran for the gate. He waited for Drù and helped close it before the two boys set off at a run for Aunt Mixele's house.

Neither boy had intended for it to become a race, but the thought of snack time spurred them on. Drù's longer legs and lighter build were a powerful advantage. He pulled ahead of Mícé. By the time he reached Aunt Mixele's patio gate, he had time to open it and wait impatiently for his friend to catch up.

Because it was grey and drizzly, everyone was inside. Drù hoped the weather would clear up by tomorrow. He liked outdoor crafts better than indoor ones.

The two friends shut the gate and walked across Aunt Mixele's patio to her door, where she met them with a hug each. Then they set their backpacks down with the others and followed her to the kitchen, where she had peaches and pumpkin cookies for all the children.

Drù could see why she'd called them. There were more crumbs than cookies on the tray, and the bowl of peaches only had six left.

Drù turned and hugged Aunt Mixele.

She laughed and hugged him back, then gave him and Mícé plates for their cookies and peaches.

Drù and Mícé took their plates over to the big table in the great room, where Lùc had been saving space for them on the bench. Aunt Mixele poured them some milk.

"Thank you," Drù remembered to say when she finished.

"Thank you," Mícé echoed.

"You're welcome, boys," she said, smiling at them. "Does anyone else need more milk?"

Lùc and a few of their other classmates asked for more. Mícé drank half of his while she was pouring the milk and asked for seconds, but Drù only wanted one glass when it was white milk. He preferred chocolate or maple milk.

"Where were you guys?" Lùc asked as soon as the thank you's had quieted down.

"We went to the garden," Drù said.

"To check on the pumpkins," Mícé added.

"I wanted to come!" Lùc grinned.

"You ran off with Bobé and Jóé instead," Mícé said.

"Yes, well," Lùc said. "I didn't want them to eat all the cookies before I got here!"

"Shhhh!" Drù giggled, louder than Mícé had been. "They'll send us back to bed!"

The boys managed a few more steps before Mícé stepped on his blanket and had to grab for the railing.

They both erupted into giggles but stilled themselves quickly when a rustling noise upstairs made the worry that they were about to get caught.

After a few tense moments, the boys continued down the stairs until they stood in the middle of the great room, looking up at the Christmas tree.

Like all the main lights in the house, the lights on the Christmas tree had been faded till they barely glowed. But to the boys' eyes, it shone with a magic that seemed proof that Santa was real.

There was no doubt that he would soon arrive. They only had to find a good place to hide until then.

They looked around.

The sofa where they always sat was very tempting, but Santa would be sure to see them there. Or Mama and Daddy might, if they came downstairs.

Drù loved laying under the Christmas tree and looking up at the lights, but there were way too many presents under there now for either of the boys to fit. And Santa would be sure to see them when he came.

The only place he could think of was the big table. He pointed.

Mícé nodded.

They ran over to the table and had barely scooted onto the bench when they dissolved into giggles.

But the bench was hard, and they couldn't see the tree unless they were sitting up.

It was going to be a long night.

Then Mícé slid off the bench, trailing his blanket.

Drù slid off after him.

The table made a perfect tent. Its legs were way off on the sides, and the tablecloth came down so low that a grownup would have to bend way over to see them. But they could see the tree and everything from their hiding place. There was even plenty of room to pile their blankets into big, soft nests.

"This is perfect!" Drù grinned.

"We'll see Santa for sure under here!" Mícé whispered loudly.

The boys giggled as they snuggled in to watch for Santa, their eyes on the tree.

"*...When the snow lay roundabout,*" Santa sang boldly as he stepped away from the seldom-used fireplace, where several split logs awaited the next cold snap, "*deep and crisp and e-ven.*"

This was truly his favorite time of year, even though fewer and fewer families remembered to share their blessings.

"*Brightly shone the moon that night,*" he continued, his deep bass reverberating through the upper reaches of the family's great room, "*though the frost was cru-el.*"

This family was different, though.

"*When a poor man came in sight, gath'ring winter fu-u-el.*"

Even in poor years, they had shared what they had.

"*Hither page and stand by me, if thou know'st it, tell me.*"

And now that they were doing well, they always left a bounty that would make little Marie proud of her children.

"*Yonder peasant, who is he? Where and what his dwelling?*"

This year was certainly no exception. There were enough new toys and clothes to brighten many poor families' Christmas, and they weren't cheap toys, either. Something told him that many of these toys were the same types that would be back under the tree later in the season.

"*Sire, he lives a good league hence, underneath the mountain.*"

And of course, there were two young boys fast asleep under the table, where they had hidden to watch for him. Now visions of sugarplums danced in their heads, and he would leave them there. This time.

"*Right against the forest fence, by Saint Agnes' fou-oun-tain.*"

Santa opened his sack, belting out his favorite lyrics.

"*Bring me flesh, and bring me wine, bring me pine logs hither. Thou and I will see him dine, when we bear them thi-ther.*"

The presents rose toward his sack, each radiating a subtle golden glow.

"*Page and monarch, forth they went, forth they went together, through the rude wind's wild lament, and the bitter wea-eh-ther.*"

One at a time, the presents swirled into the open bag, each giving a burst of red and green sparkles amid the golden light as it passed the event horizon of the bag's mouth.

"*Sire, the night is darker now, and the wind blows stronger. Fails my heart, I know not how, I can go no lon-ger.*"

The last of the presents were now rising toward the sack's fur-edged mouth. Santa's mouth spread into a bemused grin to think of what it would look like now to the boys if they had hidden behind the presents and what they would think when they awoke to see their hiding place had vanished.

"Mark my footsteps, good my page, tread thou in them boldly. Thou shalt find the winter's rage freeze thy blood less co-old-ly."

A teddy bear Drù had helped his dear mama pick out a few weeks ago gave off a veritable cascade of red and green sparkles, like the finale of an Independence Day firework display.

The amount of thought and love Drù had put into choosing a gift for a stranger warmed Santa's heart like a mugful of hot cocoa.

"In his master's steps he trod, where the snow lay dinted. Heat was in the very sod which the saint had pri-in-ted," Santa belted out with increased gusto.

Now came his favorite part of any visit.

"Therefore, all good folk, be sure, wealth or rank possessing."

With a twist of his fingers, Santa pulled a small pinch of the bright magic that surrounded him into solid form, then wafted the first two striped canes which coalesced toward the two sleeping boys. The other six canes tucked themselves into the outer branches of the tree.

"Ye who now will bless the poor, shall yourselves find ble-eh-sing."

Lecsé woke slowly, the soft light coming in the window a pleasant reminder that today was a holiday. She stretched in the soft cocoon of the bed she shared with her husband, content with the feel of his body relaxed against hers.

A family holiday. The best kind.

The soft patter of little feet warned her that her peace would be fleeting. She waited as she heard Lilée Anne tiptoe quietly down the stairs. A few minutes later, Matté scooted down the stairs, still bumping down each step on his diapered butt. Denése took the stairs slowly, one foot at a time.

She opened her eyes, to see that Sam was more awake than his relaxed embrace had led her to believe.

"Good morning, beautiful," he said, his eyes crinkling as he smiled at her.

"Good morning," she sighed happily.

"I haven't heard the boys either," he said.

"They must have stayed up very late!" she laughed. "Nothing else could keep them asleep this long."

"We can give them a little more time," Sam said, kissing her.

Half an hour later, they still hadn't heard the boys. It was time to get up, whether they wanted to or not.

She sighed and stretched luxuriatingly, smiling up at her husband.

"Are you ready to get up?" she asked. "See what the kids are up to?"

The children were playing quietly when she and Sam got downstairs. Lilée Anne was curled up on the sofa, reading one of her chapter books with a fleece throw draped over her feet the way she liked. Matté was playing with his blocks in the middle of the floor, while Denése lay under the Christmas tree looking up at the lights, right where the presents had been until Santa came for them at some point last night.

She'd been married to Sam for nearly a decade now, and it still amazed her that her wonderful but very, very *normal* husband was in a family that had such a long history with Santa. Idly, she wondered how many other families had a similar secret history with Santa.

But she really needed to figure out where the boys had disappeared to, just in case they'd gotten themselves into trouble somehow.

Lecsé looked around, but she didn't see Drù and Mícé anywhere. She glanced over at the patio door, but it still glowed a muted green, signaling that it was securely locked.

"Go check upstairs," she whispered to Sam, giving him a quick kiss. "I'll check the kitchen."

It wouldn't be the first time she'd found Drù in the kitchen, though the time he'd tried to boil an egg in the microwave had been an unpleasant experience. Even though Galatéa, the house AI, had turned off the microwave and called her as soon as it registered the issue, she'd treated the egg like unexploded ordinance till well after it was safely at room temperature again and had given him a lesson on kitchen safety that had covered everything they'd given him permissions to access. The lesson certainly hadn't scared him out of the kitchen, though between it and the tighter controls she and Sam put on his kitchen permissions, it was the last time he'd inadvertently made an explosive device.

He and Mícé weren't in here either.

She checked the hall to the garage and basement, the foyer, and the library, but there were no signs of the boys and no exterior doors glowing red. Coming back to the main room, she almost stepped on two candy canes that someone had already taken off the tree only to abandon, but she still saw no sign of the boys.

Sam came downstairs while she was standing next to the dining table, trying to think where else the boys might be.

He shook his head slowly. They weren't upstairs, either.

The boys weren't usually nearly this good at hiding.

With a dubious glance at the softly-glowing patio door, Lecsé woke the house AI.

"Galatéa! Where are Andrù Sabret and Mícal Kéavarel?" she asked.

"Andrù Sabret and Mícal Kéavarel are asleep under the dining table," Galatéa answered in her artificially feminine voice, modulated to make the listener feel calm and cared-for. "They are located approximately 0.4 meters from your current location."

"Under the— !" Lecsé exclaimed, bending over to look under the tablecloth.

Sure enough, there they were, curled up atop the soft nests of their blankets.

"The presents happened, just like you said they would," Mícé sighed. "But I wish we could have seen Santa."

"We didn't prove anything," Drù said glumly. "All that proved was that *someone* took the presents away while we were asleep."

"Sure we did," Mícé countered. "The presents were gone in the morning, just like you said they'd be."

"But that's not proof," Drù said. "I always thought it was, but that could still be parents pretending to be Santa, like Lana said."

"Even though there were a lot of presents around the tree, and they had to get them all out of here while we were sleeping right there?"

"I don't think that's proof." Drù wrinkled his brows as he pondered how the scientific method could apply to their situation. "Lana said her parents can hide a bunch of presents till Christmas Eve night and put them out while she and her sibs are sleeping, so my parents should be able to hide ours and get them out of the house later."

"But where would they put them?" Mícé asked, his voice tremulous with worry. "And what would they do with them?"

"That's what worries me," Drù said. "'Cause I get some of the same presents later, at actual Christmas. We all do."

"That's... that's awful!" Mícé exclaimed. "You think they're giving you the *exact* same presents?!"

"They could be." Drù sighed, borne down by his newfound understanding. "If Lana's right. And even lying to us about it."

"Oh, wow!" Mícé exclaimed. "That's worse than them not giving away presents at all!"

"Yeah," Drù said glumly. "And Mama let me pick out a really nice teddy bear this year for a little kid like Matté. You think they're just going to give it to him?"

"You'll know what happened if they do," Mícé said sadly. "But they *could* take them to one of those collection bins like at the big stores."

"They could," Drù agreed. "That would be better, even if it means there's no Santa."

"We have to find another way to prove he's real," Mícé said solemnly.

"Before the holiday's over," Drù agreed.

"Boys!" Lecsé called up the stairs. "Breakfast is ready!"

"Oh, good!" Drù exclaimed, the difficulty of proving Santa real temporarily forgotten. "Mama always makes the best breakfast!"

"But— " Mícé was less quick to give up on the problem.

"Come on!" Drù said, taking Mícé's arm. "Breakfast'll be great!"

Lilée Anne had beaten them to the table, even though she'd taken the time to help get Denése there.

She was sometimes annoyingly good at the big sister thing, but at least she didn't try to big sister him anymore.

Drù turned around to see if he could get Matté, but Daddy already had him. So he scooted onto the bench beside Mícé, who scooted a little closer to Lilée Anne to make room.

Mama brought the great big Christmas bread pudding out to the table, while Daddy buckled Matté into his seat.

Then Daddy went into the kitchen and came out with the huge pot they always made Christmas chocolate in—or regular hot chocolate whenever he and the others were able to talk Mama and Daddy into using it. In his other hand, he carried a massive bowl full of whipped cream to go with it.

Drù wished he could someday be as strong as a superhero, like Daddy was. He was pretty sure Daddy actually was a superhero, the way he could do anything and was strong enough to even lift Mama one-handed.

Mama started dishing up the bread pudding, starting with Matté's and Denése's little servings but not giving them theirs until she dished up everyone else's. Then they only got half a piece of sausage each, already cut up.

Drù was glad he was finally old enough to get his pudding right away and get a whole piece of sausage. It had taken so long for Mama and Daddy to realize how much more mature he was, now that he was five years old and no longer one of the youngest kids in regular school.

Drù took a bite of his bread pudding before Daddy even passed him his hot chocolate. He especially loved the Christmas bread pudding, so full of everything good that the tastes mixed on his tongue and every bite was a little different.

But the hot chocolate was his special favorite, especially the way Daddy made it for Christmas. It was thick and milky, with lots of especially good chocolate. Then Daddy topped it with a big dollop of whipped cream.

"You have to stir it with your candy cane before you drink it," Drù whispered to Mícé, "but not so you stir all the whipped cream into it."

"Okay," Mícé said, unwrapping his candy cane.

He stirred more of his whipped cream into his chocolate than Drù did, but that was fine.

Drù laughed and used his candy cane like a spoon, to scoop a big dollop of whipped cream into his mouth.

Mícé laughed and copied him.

Mama laughed.

"Just don't spill it," she said. "Or you'll be drinking from a sippy cup again."

Drù was pretty sure Mama was kidding, but he was especially careful not to spill a drop. He wasn't a baby.

He had almost finished his bread pudding and was sucking down the last chocolaty dregs of his cocoa when he realized how he and Mícé could prove that Santa was real.

Dad's cookie jar was the most amazing thing he had ever seen. It looked like any other family's Christmas cookie jar, covered in bright red holly berries and dark green leaves. But Dad had gotten it from Granddad Sabret long ago, and he'd been given it by Santa himself. Back then, Grandma Sabret had owned the pretty enameled mistletoe ornament that Aunt Mixele had now. Grandma and Granddad Sabret always got really kissy whenever they told that story. The cookie jar had something to do with the fact that they'd gotten married and had Aunt Mixele and Daddy, though Drù didn't really understand how.

But the most marvelous thing about Daddy's cookie jar was that it made any kind of cookie you could think of. Every year when they got out all the great Christmas stuff, Daddy let them try new cookie ideas and see if they liked them. Mama got some of her ideas from books, but they still usually turned out good.

Nobody else had a cookie jar that could do anything like that. They couldn't, because nobody else had a cookie jar from Santa. Nobody but Santa could even give someone a cookie jar like it, because nobody else could do magic.

There. He'd just used the scientific method to prove that Santa was real. He just had to prove it to Mícé.

"Here," Drù said. "Have a cookie."

Mícé reached for the cookie Drù held out to him, then stopped.

"Is it peanut butter?" he asked, uncertain.

Drù turned his hand to look more closely at the cookie.

"I think so," he said. "It looks like them, and I know Daddy really likes them."

"I don't." Mícé made a face. "Mom makes us peanut butter sandwiches all the time. I don't like how it tastes, or how it sticks to the roof of my mouth. Is there anything else?"

Drù's eyes went wide. His free hand flew to his mouth.

"I forgot!" he exclaimed. "Mama said I should always ask my guests what type of cookies they like, 'cause not everyone likes every type of cookies like I do."

"Anything but peanut butter," Mícé said, grimacing. "What else do you have?"

"That's not the way our cookie jar works," Drù said, grinning widely. "I can get you pretty much any type of cookie you like."

Mícé knew Drù's mommy and daddy cooked a lot, but he didn't think they would have *every* type of cookie anyone ever made. So he tried to think of the strangest type of cookie he'd ever heard of.

"Snickers-doobles?" he said uncertainly.

"Okay," Drù said. "Watch."

He put the peanut butter cookie on his plate, then went back to the counter where the cookie jar was.

Drù stepped up on the stool and lifted the lid off the cookie jar. He carefully put it down on the counter beside the cookie jar. Then he looked in. Daddy's cookie jar was more than half full, and all the cookies were his peanut butter cookies.

"You should look too," he said, looking over his shoulder at Mícé.

Mícé stepped up onto the stool beside Drù and looked down into the cookie jar.

"They're all peanut butter cookies," he said. He sounded disappointed.

"That's okay," Drù said. He hoped he was right. "Think about snickers-doobles."

Drù closed his eyes and thought really hard about Mícé's snickers-doobles. He thought about how much he wanted to find out how the strange-sounding cookies tasted. They were probably better hot, but not too hot. Mama didn't let him have cookies when they first came out of the oven, because they were so hot he'd burn himself.

Drù didn't want his cookies to be that hot. Burns hurt.

He hoped the snickers-doobles weren't one of those cookies with icing. Icing would melt off the hot cookies.

He was getting distracted. He needed to just think about a fresh batch of snickers-doobles.

He scrunched up his nose, saying "snickers-doobles" over and over.

Then he opened his eyes.

Mícé was staring at him.

He looked back at Mícé. Then he looked at the cookie jar.

It looked the same. But the cookie smell had changed. Now it smelled like cinnamon and butter.

There was only one thing to do. He looked in the jar, at the cookies.

They weren't Daddy's peanut butter cookies. Now they were thick, golden cookies with some sort of golden powder on them.

He hoped they were snickers-doobles.

Mícé looked in the cookie jar.

He looked back at Drù.

"How'd you do that?" he asked Drù.

"I just thought about your snickers-doobles," Drù said. "Are these snickers-doobles?"

"I don't know," Mícé said. "I just thought the name sounded cool. But they're not the same cookies that were in there."

"That's because Daddy's cookie jar is magic," Drù said.

"It's not a normal cookie jar, that's for sure," Mícé said. "Ours only holds cookies that someone made. It doesn't change the cookies to something else. How does it do that?"

"Daddy says Granddad got it straight from Santa. The Santa magic makes it work."

"So this proves Santa's real?"

"I think so," Drù said. "I don't know any other way the cookies could change like that."

"Neither do I," Mícé said. "But we should try them, just to make sure."

The boys grinned at each other. Then they reached into the cookie jar and each took out a hot—but not too hot—snickers-doobles cookie.

Santa was real, after all. No doubt about it.

Santa Paws is Real?

By Sarah Arnette

"I'm too old to believe in Santa Paws," Mabel says as she trots next to her brother, me, Andrew. Mabel is excited to see the winter lights decorating the neighborhood houses, but she feels her brother teasing her about Santa Paws is going a little too far.

"You are never too old to believe in Santa Paws," I tell her as we stroll down the sidewalk. I turn to look at her as I talk to her. She looks adorable with her pink hat on, and pink plaid jacket with the cream-colored shirring. She even has on little pink boots. I almost can't see any of the little pitbull that is struggling under her winter gear. It is too cute.

I am not dressed that much differently from Mabel. My outfit was hunter green, though. I also do not need quite as much protection from the weather. I am a German Shepherd, and my fur is a lot thicker than hers. The main difference between the two of us is that I am confident and graceful in my outfit. I owe it all to my advanced intelligence and sense of poise. Oh, and I'm older than she is.

My brother, Tommy, is dressed in a cute Santa jacket, matching boots, and a hat. He is a Boston Terrier mix, and since he is so small, Mom even put leg warmers on him. She made Dad promise to carry him if the snow gets too deep. There is no dignity in this family.

Mom is staying home with Amilia. She has gotten too old to risk being out in the freezing cold for some winter lights. Dad promised to take lots of pictures for both of them to look at when we got home. Mom really likes the lights, but she is not a fan of the cold. She says that if her family were not all here, we would all move to the south, where they do not get six feet of snow in a single day. Mom would miss the snow if we left it behind.

"Santa Paws is just a story that parents tell their pups so that they will behave," Mabel continues. She sounds so sure of herself. It is hard to believe that she's not a puppy anymore, but rather a growing young adult. How did that happen? At least she will never be older than me, ha!

"Lies, Santa Paws is real. I bet some pups in your school told you that because they don't get any gifts from him because they are bad," Tommy pipes up for the first time. I almost couldn't hear him with the red scarf Mom wrapped around his face. His face is not quite as flat as most Boston Terriers, but he can have a hard time breathing every now and again, especially when his nose gets too cold.

"If he is real, how come no one has ever seen him?" Mabel argues. Oh, we're onto the logic game now? Poor pup, we're gonna win this one, and she is going to be so confused by the time we are done that she will have no choice but to believe in Santa Paws for another year.

"Magic," Tommy answers, as if it is the most obvious thing in the world. That was not the answer I was going to go with. I was planning to talk about the different space-time continua, string theory, and time dilation. Instead, we are apparently going with the "Magic" answer.

"Magic. You expect me to believe that magic exists and that Santa Paws uses magic to keep himself hidden," Mabel sounds disbelieving. I don't really blame her. The whole thing sounds made up when you use an explanation like that one.

"Yep, magic. Any advanced enough science can be described as magic, and in this instance, the science is so advanced that it might as well be magic. Arthur C. Clarke said that," Tommy answers. I actually think that is a good answer. That way, we don't have to explain the science because it is too advanced for us, and anything we say that sounds like magic is automatically presented as advanced science.

"Right..."Mabel drawls. Luckily for us, the first houses on the route are coming up. They are so bright that we could see them half a block away.

"What is that song that they are playing?" Tommy asks. He cannot really hear very well, on account of being wrapped up tight in a scarf with dog earmuffs under his hat. Mom tried to put those on me, and I just looked at her. There is only so far I am willing to let her take dressing me up. Tommy, on the other hand, would do anything to make Mom smile, including wearing earmuffs.

"I think it is Santa Paws is Coming to Town," Mabel answers. She knows the song very well. Mom has a small ornament that she puts on the mantle every winter that plays that song. It has a small man in red holding a small tree, though, so I am not sure what that has to do with Santa Paws.

"I think the song is, Santa Claus is Coming to Town," Dad says. He is always trying to correct us. It never works.

"Mom said it was Santa Paws, and Mom is always right," Tommy answers back. Dad just laughs at that one for some reason. Tommy is right, though, what Mom says goes, and that makes her always right.

As we approach the house, the song repeats itself. It does not look like it will switch songs the entire time we are there. The whole house is decorated with men in big red suits. They are all carrying big bags or have big bags filled with toys at their feet. There are light-up reindeer, as well. They are attached to a giant sled.

"Okay, so Santa Paws uses magic to get around without being seen. Let's say I buy it. How does he get the reindeer to fly? Deer do not fly," Mabel quips. Santa Paws flies around in a big sleigh pulled by reindeer. The deer all have silly names, but that seems to be pretty common in the pet world. We have normal names, but our neighbors have names like Noodle and Egg. Our other neighbors are named Max, Brutus, Circe, and No One. Yeah, humans are weird.

"They are obviously not real deer. They are animatronic deer that defy gravity and move super fast. The science is super complicated and therefore fits in the magic category," I answer. I can't let Tommy control the entire story. He will get lost, and the next thing we know, Mabel will be back to not believing in Santa Paws.

"Right..."Mable drawls again.

The next house we went to did not have music playing, which was good. It would not have sounded nice to have two different songs competing for our attention. Instead, this house went simple. The whole house and the various trees in the yard were decorated with white lights.

"I could almost believe in magic, looking at how the lights reflect off the snow and ice," Mabel says, almost too quietly to be heard, but I heard her and smiled.

The next few houses were dark. They all had some type of winter decorations, but they were not lit. Some of them had ornaments hanging from their porches, and a lot of them had signs with a friendly old man on them. Most of the signs have writing on them, but I can't read, so I don't know what they say. I am a dog, after all.

The next house with winter lights is playing an old Christian song called "Silent Night." This house is decorated with a manger and plastic people gathered around a baby. I don't know what the scene is showing me, but it looks peaceful. The donkey seems like it is ready to take a nap. I like it.

There are many houses along the route, and it is a lot of fun. The best home is the one where they have a walkway set up that takes us all the way to the back of the house. They gave Dad a cup of hot cider, and they gave us some water to drink and some puppy cookies. Mabel, who was looking a little tired up until that moment, perked right up and was very excited for the cookie.

We even saw Brutus, Max, Circe, and No One there. They were traveling with the dogs from down the street, Han Solo and Leia. We got to runaround and play in the snow for a while. I showed Mabel how to make snow angels. Max, a big mastiff of a dog, helped Tommy climb on a snowman so he could jump into the soft snow. It was so much fun.

On the way home, it began to snow. It started snowing very heavily, and Dad had us stay close to him. Tommy had a hard time with the snow, and Dad had to pick him up. I broke the path, pushing through the snow. Mabel followed right behind me, with Dad taking the rear with Tommy. It was tough going. Dad kept trying to take the lead. He said he was bigger and could break the snow better, but he only had two feet, and he was carrying Tommy. I insisted I could do it.

After what seemed like hours of trudging in the snow, but really could not have been that long, I saw our house. Mom was standing at the window, a worried expression on her face. Amilia was in her arms, and she looked equally as concerned. I don't know why they would be worried. We did not go far, and I can always find my way home.

We did not even make it to the door before Mom had it open and ushered us inside. The blast of warmth from the house was such a change from the icy outside that I just stood there for a moment. This gave Mom enough time to get my clothes off me and dry my legs and feet. She checked them for frostbite and finally let me sit in front of the fireplace. Mabel followed right behind me, tucking into my side and falling asleep.

When we woke up, the living room had been transformed. Last night, when we lay down in front of the fireplace, the living room looked like it always did. It had a television in the corner and two couches set up to bracket it, giving everyone a good angle to watch TV. The dining room is right off the living room, and usually has a small table and a couple of rocking chairs. We don't use that room very often.

This morning, everything changed. The furniture was the same in the living room, but all the blankets had been changed out to look like mounds of snow. The dining room table had been moved clear out of the room and replaced with a tree. The rocking chairs were there, but they were now decorated with snowflake pillows. The best part was that there were presents piled everywhere. Santa Paws had come!

"When did this happen?" Mabel asks, blinking her eyes awake.

"It happened while we were sleeping," I answer her. It is the most obvious answer possible. When else could it have happened?

"Okay, but how did this happen?"

"Um...Magic," is the only answer I can give her. To be honest, I have no idea how this happened. This seems like an awful lot of work for someone to have done without waking either of us up. The tree is really only a couple of feet away from me. I should have heard someone removing the table and putting up a tree. Plus, it is decorated!

"Magic..."Mabel repeats. She does not sound quite so disbelieving this time. After all, it is hard to argue with your own eyes.

Shortly after we woke up, everyone else woke up. They all slept upstairs, in their beds. I admit that might have been more comfortable than sleeping on the floor, but the fireplace was warm. At some point, the fire had been banked, but there was still warmth radiating from it. It could not have been banked that long ago.

Mom and Dad look a little tired, but everyone else is very excited. Apparently, no one knew about the decor change or how the tree got there. Tommy and Amilia were very eager to rip open their presents, but Mom and Dad said they had to wait until breakfast. Mabel tried to sneak a present, but Dad had raised me first, so he was onto her tricks before she was even aware she had the idea.

Mom usually serves us our specialized foods. It is always a kibble, but each of us needs different things, so we have our own bags of dogfood. Today, Mom added an over-easy egg and a pumpkin cookie to our food. I really wanted to take my time and enjoy the treats, but I was too excited to slow down. I still did not beat Mabel, though. I don't think she even took a breath as she ate her food. Tommy finished right after me, and that left us all waiting on Amelia.

She took her time eating her food, making sure all her kibble was coated with egg yolk before even starting. I was a little worried that Mabel was going to collapse in anticipation or rush over and eat Amelia's food for her. Eventually, she finished, then waited a full thirty seconds before taking a drink of water and stepping away from the bowl. That last bit was unnecessary, I think.

Finally, we were allowed to go into the dining room and open presents. I might not know how to read, but I can identify my name. I found the pile with my name on it and began to sniff through it, trying to find just the right present to open. I stopped when I saw Mabel staring at her pile. She was simply too overwhelmed.

This was Mabel's first winter celebration. She had never received a Santa Paws present before, so she did not know where to start or what to do. She could smell all the fun things, but they were wrapped in shiny paper. No wonder she had convinced herself that Santa Paws was not real. If he wasn't real, he could not forget to give her a present. One day, she will realize that she really is part of this family, forever.

I sniffed my pile once again and selected a likely-smelling package. I took it over to her and showed her what I picked up. She hunted through her pile until she found a similar package. Dropping onto my belly, I held my present in my front paws and began to rip at the paper with my front teeth, being careful not to use my canines. I did not want to damage the present; I just wanted to remove the paper. I will admit, I had a lot of fun shredding the paper into tiny pieces.

Once the paper was destroyed, I found myself holding a brand-new nylon bone. This one smelled like lamb and promised to be a lot of fun to chew on. Mabel, who had watched my technique, was having a blast ripping up the paper. She was even more astonished to find that she, too, had a nylon bone. This one smelled like peanut butter, which is one of her favorite foods.

Mabel's eyes were huge when she looked at this new toy. "This is mine?" she said in a hushed voice. It was almost as though she was expecting someone to come along and take it away from her and tell her that everything was an elaborate joke on her.

"It had your name on it, right?" I ask her.

"Yeah. It said Mabel, right on the front. All of these do," she answered, indicating the rest of the pile of presents in front of her.

"Then yes, it is all yours. You do not need to share it with anyone if you don't want to," I answer. I resolved not to steal it from her. This is her first winter present. I will leave it alone. All the rest of her winter presents after this year, those are open game. I am her older brother, after all.

"You can use it if you want," she offers, looking up at me. Oh, she is too precious. I love my little sister.

"Open the rest of your presents, silly," I tell her as I stand up, bopping her on the top of her head lightly. As I walk to my pile of presents, I see her pounce on her gifts, scattering them around her. She is having the best time in her little life.

Santa Paws got everyone exactly what they most wanted. I got a lot of chew toys. I love chew toys. I am pretty sure that I have every type of nylon chew toy ever made. I also got some treats and wet food. Mom opened up a couple of the treat bags for me and let me have a couple of treats. She said I could not eat them all at once, as it would make my tummy hurt. I believe her because once I got into a whole package of hot dogs, and my tummy wasn't happy after that.

Tommy got clothes. He loves dressing up and looking all spiffy. He got acute sailor's outfit, hat included. He also got a new jacket and some new boots. His treats looked just like mine, but they were smaller. I think that is because he has a smaller mouth than I do.

Amilia got a new bed and some wet food. She also has a sweater and some treats. She did not get any chew toys because she does not like to chew on things anymore. Her favorite thing to do is lounge on her bed and be cuddled. Mom even got a Santa Paws present for her and Amilia. It is a sweatshirt that Mom can wear and use to carry Amilia around. I know they are both going to love that.

Mabel got toys. There were so many toys in her pile. She got balls, stuffies, nylon chew toys, ropes... if it was in the toy aisle, she got it, it looks like. It could have been an optical illusion, though. She had spread all her toys around and kept grabbing one after another, as though she was undecided about what to play with. She might be a young adult dog, but at that moment, she looked like little puppy. It was not long before she passed out, sound asleep, in the middle of a pile of toys, with a plush stuffed deer in her mouth.

When Mabel finally wakes up, I show her something I found while she had been napping. There, coming from the fireplace, and back to it, were paw prints. They were smaller than you would have expected from anyone in the family, except for Amilia. They were also cat tracks, and they still bore the white frostings that looked suspiciously like snow.

"What is this?" Mabel asks as she bends down to sniff at the tracks. They make their way to the tree and then back again, avoiding where she and I had been sleeping the night before.

"They appear to be Santa Paws' tracks. Do you see the magic snow surrounding the tracks?" I point out the "snow." It looks like glitter, or maybe that spray frost Mom sometimes uses on the windows, once I take a closer look. I am not mentioning that to Mabel, and I am hoping she does not notice it.

"Santa Paws is a cat?" Mabel asks, confused.

"What? No one said Santa Paws was a dog. How would that make any sense at all, that Santa Paws was a dog? Do you think either of us could go through the chimney? That's how Santa Paws gets in the house, through the chimney. How about staying on a slanted roof? You or I would just slide right off, but a cat? A cat could do it," I answer. A cat is the only plausible explanation for Santa Paws, I know. I have thought a lot about him.

"Santa Paws... is a... cat," Mabel nods as she repeats the statement to herself. "Yeah, that makes sense. If Santa Paws were a dog, he would have gotten burnt coming down the chimney. We still had a fire going by the time I fell asleep. Although I guess he waited until someone banked it."

"I guess, I don't know. I have never managed to stay awake long enough to see Santa Paws. And he is invisible to all kinds of technology, like cameras. It is part of his super-advanced technology that rivals magic," I improvise. Mabel is brilliant; if there is a hole in the story, she'll find it.

"I've seen Santa Paws," Amilia says, drawing Mabel's attention. In moments, Mabel is sitting in front of the old chihuahua, giving her all her attention.

"What did Santa Paws look like?"

"Santa Paws is the biggest Maine Coon cat you can ever imagine. His fur is so thick that snow and ice cannot touch him. His ears are tufted, and he wears his tail like a scarf when he sits in his sleigh. His coat is a red brindle, and he wears a thick quilted flying jacket. He hides his eyes behind green flying goggles, but when I met him, he raised them, showing me the palest of green eyes.

"He can decorate an entire room with nothing but the twitch of his tail. He has spies to tell him if you have been good or bad all year, and he rewards or punishes you accordingly. You must have been extra good this year, you got a lot of presents. Andrew did not get as many, and that is because he can be a challenge for Mom and Dad," Amilia told her.

"He spies on us?" Mabel questions.

"Yep, all year long. They tell him if you have been naughty or nice. If you ate your food or if you peed in the kitchen. They act just like the song says. You know the song, right? Mom played it for you, I know."

"How does he spy on us?"

"He has the squirrels watch you," Amilia squints at Mabel as she says this last part. It is enough to send Mabel into a fit of zoomies, and she tears around the house in her excitement. Squirrels watch over her and report her behavior to Santa Paws!

Some hours later, after Mom and Dad clean up all the scraps of paper, Mabel is lying next to me, chewing on her peanut-butter-flavored nylon bone. "This has been the best day ever," she announces.

"I thought the beach day was your best day ever," I say, reminding her of her previous favorite day.

"That day is also the best day ever. I can have more than one best day ever," She does not even try to argue with me about it. She continues chewing her toy for a minute, then stops. "I take that back. There is one best day ever, and it is not today. This is a best day, but there is one day that is really the best day ever."

I know what day this is. I have a similar best day ever, if I am right about what her best day ever is. "And that is?"

"My best day ever is the day that I got to come live with you guys. The day that Mom and Dad rescued me. That is my best day ever. On that day, I went from being all alone to having a Mommy and Daddy. On that day, I got three older siblings and a whole new world I could not even imagine before. That is the best day ever," she answers. She never looked up when she said this. She just stared at her toy as if she was embarrassed.

"Yeah, I have a best day ever just like that one. I got two older siblings. The second-best day ever was when they brought you home, all wrapped up in blankets and squirming to be free. Love you, little sister," I tell her, resting my front leg across her back.

Mabel rolled over and started batting at my face, almost as if she were a cat. With a couple of purposeful sneezes, she indicates that she wants to play with me, the nylon toy all but forgotten. As if I could turn my sister down on this, one of her bestest days ever.

The Eggnog Incident

By Stephanie Osborn

[This is a story in the *Gingerbread Cat* universe.]

Things were proceeding well in the wrapping room. Then again, it was only July; daylight was continuous at the North Pole this time of year, and Nikolai Krisstoffsen, aka Saint Nick or Santa Claus—the name change was a story unto itself, and involved a certain saint with which he'd been confused—tended to staff multiple shifts during the summer months, taking advantage of the extra light. The end result was around-the-clock operations, and a huge jump in development and production of toys; they got ahead of the Christmas production schedule that way.

So he popped by to see how things were going, and if all the elves had managed to adjust well to their seasonal sleep schedules; sometimes he worked shift trades between elves if someone was having problems sleeping. Ginger rode on his shoulder like usual; the smart, talkative orange cat could be very useful in working out the details. *Well, let's face it,* Santa thought: Ginger, being blessed with the ability to talk, the intelligence of an extremely smart human, and a life as long as Santa—he'd been Santa's cat since Nik was a young magus or wise man going to visit the baby Jesus in Bethlehem—was no ordinary cat. More, he was Santa's best friend. So he was expecting all to go smoothly.

What he didn't expect was the tiny elf hugging Almond Honeytree tightly. It was adorable, and he heard Ginger's little trill of delight at seeing so sweet a scene, so he headed straight for the pair.

"Hello, there, Almond," Santa's deep voice said gently, as they approached. "Who do you have with you?"

"Oh, hello, Santa," Almond said, looking up with a smile. "This is my son, Peanut. He just got out of school for the day and came to see me before going home."

Peanut looked up at the big human, and the cat riding his shoulder, and paled.

"Hello, Peanut," Santa said with a smile, offering a hand to shake. "How are you today? So you came to visit your father at work?"

Peanut stared at Santa's outstretched hand, then seemed to panic. With a cry, he spun and ran blindly across the big room toward the door on the far side, heedless of stacked Christmas packages in the way. Cries of dismay went up from the elves as boxes came crashing down. There were several sounds like glass breaking, and Ginger realized that some gifts would have to be replaced or repaired.

The little elf vanished through the door, but Ginger's sensitive ears heard what sounded like crying. He glanced at Santa.

Apparently Santa's ears heard it too, for the look in the blue eyes was concerned. Santa turned back to the father.

"What just happened, Almond?" he wondered.

"I am so, so sorry, sir!" Almond exclaimed, worried and embarrassed. "Peanut can be very shy and has gotten worse in the last year. He's only seven years old, and currently our only child, though we're planning for more; we've been working with him, but we aren't sure what's wrong, or how to fix it."

Santa nodded his understanding. "I have an idea what it might be," he noted. "I've seen it happen before. Don't worry."

"I'll go fetch him and take him home as soon as I tell my supervisor," Almond offered.

"No, no, don't interrupt your work; I caused this, so I'll figure out how to fix it. Ah! Ginger, I think you're best suited to go find the young fellow and talk to him. See if you can find out what happened and do what you need to do to settle matters. If he'll let you, I'd love to see young Peanut later... maybe somewhere neutral, where he won't be frightened."

"Okay, Santa," Ginger agreed, hopping down and heading for the far door, even as Santa moved to help the elves clean up the mess.

Ginger followed the child's scent and finally found little Peanut on the far side of the castle, huddled under a table in a corridor, crying. His ears perked in concern, and he silently moved close, until his whiskers brushed Peanut's hand, then he began purring. Peanut looked up at that.

"Oh, hi, Ginger," the little one said, sniffling a bit. "Did I make Santa mad?"

"No, but he wondered what he did to scare you. I think that kind of upset him a little, but it was more concern for you. Do you want a cuddle and some purrs?"

"Dat would be nice, yes," Peanut agreed. "I will pet oo if you will purr for me."

"Happily," Ginger said, delicately walking across the boy's legs, then settling himself against the little elf, ramping up his purring as high as it would go.

Peanut hugged him gently—Ginger was almost as big as the tiny elf child—and rested his face in Ginger's fur, letting one hand stroke through the soft reddish-orange fur.

They stayed like that until Peanut stopped crying and calmed down.

"Now," Ginger said, once he'd licked the tear stains from Peanut's face, groomed his hair and gotten him presentable again, "tell me what happened."

"I... I don't know," Peanut admitted. "I'm just... scared of Santa, sort of."

"But why? Have you seen him do something that frightens you?"
"No, neber."
"What, then? Is he so big and tall that he scares you?"
"Well, dat's a little ob it—he's so much taller than us elves—but..."
"What, then?"
"Does Santa *ever* mess up?"

"What, you mean does he make mistakes?"

"Yesh."

"Well, of course he does. He's human, after all."

"He's not an angel?"

"In a way he is, because that word 'angel' just means a messenger. He carries the message of love to children around the world. That was the mission that God gave him, you see."

"Ooo."

"But no, he makes mistakes, just like the rest of us. Is that the problem? Does he intimidate you?"

"Intim..."

"Intimidate."

"What does that mean?"

"Um... are you in awe of him?"

"You mean...?"

"Do you think so much of him that you get scared trying to figure out how to act around him?"

"YES! Dat's it, kitty! Oh, you are so smart! Yes, I wuv him an' I want him to be proud of me, but I don't know how," Peanut explained. "I only mess up instead. Like just now." He waved a tiny hand toward the Wrapping Department. "Oh, Daddy will be so mad. I heard da packages fall, heard da glass breaking. But do you know, Ginger, I never eben saw da packages?"

"Did you only see the door?"

"Yes."

"Your dad isn't mad either, Peanut," the cat told the lad. "Worried about you, yes, but not mad. Last I saw of them, he and Santa were going to help clean up and see what needed to be replaced." Ginger paused, then added, "And don't worry. Santa always has backups for his gifts. He always has at least two of everything made. This isn't the first time there's been breakage in the production line. Sometimes it's somebody bumping a stack of boxes, and sometimes it's the conveyor belts going haywire. Every year we have at least one such accident."

"Oh," Peanut sighed in tremendous relief. "Dat's good. It isn't just me, and Santa has backup plans."

"Yes, he does. Would it help if I told you about a time when everything messed up, on Christmas Eve, at that? I mean, EVERYTHING messed up!"

"Ohhh," Peanut sighed, eyes going round. "No, no, no! On Christmas Eve?! Dat's bad!"

"Yup," Ginger chuckled. "I never thought we'd pull that one off."

"Yesh, tell me, please!"

"All right," Ginger said, thinking. "This was many, many years ago; I think only Santa's family will remember it now..."

"An' you're in Santa's family?" Peanut asked.

"Yes, I've been beside him since before he met Mrs. Claus," Ginger said with a cat's grin. "That's a long story itself. But *this* story starts off with Mrs. Claus getting a new recipe for egg nog. You know how they all like egg nog."

"Evvybody likes egg nog!" Peanut laughed.

"Well, not everybody, but almost everybody at the North Pole sure does." Ginger's grin grew wider. "I've even been known to lap a bowl of it now and then, though Mrs. Claus insists it must be what she calls 'virgin,' meaning no rum, which is bad for us kitties."

"Dat's how us kids drink it, too. Though last year Momma and Daddy let me taste some of theirs—it was Christmas Day, not Christmas Eve, though. It was good, but it burned, sort of."

"Right. That's the alcohol. And this recipe called for a lot more rum than the usual adult version, and had a lot more sugar in it..."

"Honey, dinner was delicious," Nikolai Krisstoffsen Claus, Der Kringler—Santa Claus himself—told his wife Zara bas Abram-Krisstoffsen; her brother Noam bar Abram, chief toy designer, nodded agreement. "That was possibly the best Christmas Eve dinner we've ever had."

"And this egg nog is delicious!" Noam agreed, refilling his mug for the second time with the spiced rum punch.

"Careful there, brother, it's a potent beverage this year!" Zara said with a laugh. "I love that new recipe, but I think next year I'll only put in half the rum it calls for, especially on top of the brandy and Irish cream!"

"Whoa!" Noam said, staring into his mug. "No wonder it tastes so strong!"

"It's really good, though," Santa agreed. "This'll keep me warm through the whole ride!"

"Do you want me to fix you an insulated coffee container of it to take with you? Or do you want hot cocoa or plain coffee instead?"

"I think hot cocoa will be fine," Santa decided. "Maybe with a *very* light nip of brandy. Let's save what's left of the egg nog until I get home. We can celebrate the holiday with it."

"Okay. I'll wait up for you like usual," she told him, and they kissed as he rose from the table. He tripped over a chair leg and staggered for a moment, then got his balance and chuckled. "Grace personified, that's me. All right, let me go supervise loading the sleigh, and I'll head out. Stay warm, my love."

"Always, Nik," Zara said with a smile. "Be careful. I love you."

"I love you, too, and I will be. By the way, Noam, that new doll design is perfect; you did great!"

"Thanks, Nik," Noam said with a smile, still sipping his third mug of egg nog. "Safe travel. HaShem be beside you."

"Thank you, brother," Santa said, nodding, and headed out.

But Santa tripped twice—apparently over the perfectly flat carpeting—on his way to the sleigh hangar.

When he arrived, he found the elf team charged with putting the reindeer into their harnesses was... a little confused.

Santa had long since developed the order of harnessing these special flying deer; his father, the previous Der Kringler, or chief magician to what was then the Viking king (even if half the Vikings ignored what he said), had created the magick that made them fly. The deer were not as long-lived as the Claus family, but the flying magick bred true, and so over the years, the harness positions—and likewise, the deer who were placed there—took on the names of those original eight deer on the pull team: Dasher, Dancer, Prancer, Vixen, Comet, Cupid, Donder, and Blitzen.

Unfortunately, the deer—who were trained for certain spots in harness—were not in that order. They were in reverse order except for Vixen and Cupid, whose places were exchanged in the reverse lineup. More, at least three of them were backward in the harnesses. How on earth *that* had happened, Santa had no idea. He aimed straight for the team lead, Oliver 'Lucky' Cloverleaf.

"Lucky, what in the name of the Star of Bethlehem is going on here?"

"Uh? Santa? Whatsh da matter?" The elf spun, then staggered slightly, recovering quickly.

"The deer are all out of order!" Santa exclaimed. "Your team even managed to get Prancer, Vixen, and Blitzen into the leathers backward! Take them all out of harness and get it right! Weren't you paying attention??"

"Payin' 'tention to what, now?"

That was when Santa got a whiff of Lucky's breath.

"Oh, HaShem help us," he murmured, suddenly understanding. "Lucky, did you have egg nog with your Christmas Eve dinner?"

"Sure did," the team lead declared with a huge grin. "It 'uz good! I had three mugs!"

"And the other elves?"

"Kept up wi' me," Lucky declared. "Please tell Mrs. Claus she done real good, sir. We usually have t' add a wee bit more rum t' our egg nog to get it to our liking, and the cafeteria cooks just go on and add it t' whatever Mrs. Claus sends down. But this time, they all nailed it! When the cafeteria cooks got done, it was perfect!" He stepped toward Santa and nearly fell.

Oh dear, Santa thought. *Rum AND brandy AND Irish cream... and they added MORE rum, because Zara is usually very light-handed with alcohol. My elves are all drunk and didn't have a clue.* Then he considered the way he'd tripped over the perfectly smooth carpet in the corridor—twice—and realized they might not be the only ones; he didn't have the stamina or constitution of an elf, after all. *Oh no,* he groaned to himself.

"Lucky, go sit down," he said then, pointing at the nearest chair he saw. "And stay put."

"Yes, sir," Lucky said, turning, nearly falling again, then wobbling over to the chair and sitting down on it. Santa turned to the sleigh team.

"EVERYONE STOP WHAT YOU'RE DOING AND SIT DOWN WHERE YOU ARE!" he roared across the hangar, and activity ceased as elves sat on the floor and turned their attention to him.

The slight, warm fuzzy he'd had in the back of his mind faded away as realization hit him that this had happened on the worst possible night, at the worst possible time. He wasn't sure how to fix matters, because chances were good that his entire preparations staff, from Final Packing to Stowage to Launch, were likely in as bad a shape as Lucky and his Sleigh Prep team. He shook his head, then tried the only thing he could think of.

"Is there anybody in here who doesn't like egg nog, and didn't have any with dinner?"

Half a dozen hands went up.

"Good. This is important, so listen carefully. The egg nog had far more alcohol in it than it should have, thanks to Mrs. Claus trying a new recipe, and the cafeteria assuming it would be too weak and adding more. I want you six to RUN to the cafeteria and tell them to crank out some urns of coffee, as strong as they can make it, and then take an urn to each department, and have all the elves drink several cups each. NO SUGAR. I need everyone clear-headed, or we're going to really mess up Christmas this year. And Winky? Winky Bean? Is that you, there?"

"Yes, sir!"

"Good. Fetch me back a big mug of black coffee, preferably something that's been sitting on the burner for several hours and is really strong. As fast as you can get it to me."

"But sir, that'll taste yucky!"

"Yes, it will, but I had egg nog with dinner, too, and I can't wait for cafeteria staff to brew an urn. Now you six, go, and go fast! Once everyone else is fed, the cafeteria staff will eat, and then they'll be in a mess, too. I want to catch them before that happens, if we can."

They went out at a dead run.

Five minutes later, Winky Bean was back with a huge mug of black coffee. Santa took it and began to chug it. It did indeed taste bitter and burned, but he could also tell it was strong.

As he drank, all the seated—and therefore drunk—elves began to chant, "Go! Go! Go! Go!" until the mug—it was really more a stein—was empty. Then they began to cheer. He stifled a snort that would have sent coffee out his nose and over the half-dozen nearest elves.

By the time he'd finished it, three of the other elves who didn't like egg nog were back with what Santa assumed was the partially-filled urn from which Winky had poured his coffee, and an entire stack of disposable cups.

"There's fresh coming in a few minutes, sir," Winky told him. "And we caught the cafeteria staff as they were sitting down to eat; the chef about had a herd of reindeer! He's heading up the coffee production right now. But we figured this bunch maybe needed it fast, like you, so we arranged to bring along the same urn."

"Good idea, Winky. Thank you."

The coffee, which had been in the cafeteria all afternoon for those who might need a pick-me-up, was indeed strong; Winky and his friends handed it out quickly. In short order, Lucky and his top people were starting to sober. They removed all the reindeer from the sleigh's harness, then put them in proper order and began reharnessing. Unfortunately, the three harnesses that had held the three backward reindeer had been damaged by the process, and there wasn't time left in the schedule to replace them for the simple reason that they had no replacements and would need to have the leatherworkers make new pieces of the harnesses, so they were repaired on the spot as best the team could manage.

"But it ought to be fine, sir," a very embarrassed Lucky told Santa.

"I hope so, Lucky. I surely hope so."

He made a mental note for future Christmases to always have backup harnesses for the deer.

When the cafeteria staff wheeled a cart with a fresh coffee urn into the hangar, Santa—feeling much less fuzzy in the head—refilled his stein, added a bit of cream and some cocoa, then headed for the other departments to see what was up there.

The department in the biggest mess proved to be Stowage. This was where all the packages were placed into the enormous, magickal 'bags of holding' that Santa used on his sleigh. They were much bigger on the inside than the outside, and often a small staff of elves rode inside each one to ensure the gifts were offloaded at the right house, but they still had to be packed just so, and not, for instance, place gifts going to Great Britain in the same bag with gifts for children in the United States. Each continent had its own bag—there was even a small one for Antarctica, for the scientists who lived there—and within each big bag were smaller bags that represented geographic areas.

Unfortunately, under the influence of the very strong egg nog, the locations had been all mixed up, and the elves were quickly emptying the bags to re-sort them and get them into the proper bags. Santa hadn't been involved in developing the sorting system they used, and this was before the invention of scanning codes, so he helped by using his time magick—the same magick he used to ensure everything was delivered overnight, around the world—to slow down the clock and give them more time to do the job.

In the end, the sleigh launched only twenty minutes late for its around-the-world mission. This was of no concern, however; that was well within Santa's ability to counter with his magicks. He had been an excellent pupil under the Magi as well as his father, the high wizard of the Vikings, many centuries ago, and he had been blessed by the risen Christ some two thousand years ago. So within moments they had made up the time, and were flying down the International Date Line, where Christmas Eve first began changing to Christmas Day, stopping along the way to deliver packages, then moving ever farther west, toward Asia.

They hadn't made it to Australia yet when Prancer, in the second rank of deer, got sick.

Very sick.

The poor deer started by losing control of her bowels, pelting deer scat on the team behind him. This was met with grunts and snorts of displeasure by the rest of the team... until poor Prancer developed diarrhea.

This resulted in most of the team lunging this way and that as they sought to avoid the liquid waste, and Santa had a hard time keeping control. It also put additional strain on the harness, because the reindeer didn't all move in the same direction to avoid the splatter.

It was exacerbated moments later when Prancer began to throw up.

Reindeer weren't supposed to be able to do that.

"Okay, that does it," Santa said, pulling on the reins to slow his team and begin a descent. "I need to find a place to land, doctor Prancer, then send someone back home with her. Winky?" he called to the nearest open sack of gifts, and an elf head popped out of its mouth. "Who's our best bareback rider on board?"

"Um, that's gonna be Berry Bramblebush, I think, sir."

"Get her up here. I'm putting down. Prancer's really sick."

"Do you know what's wrong?"

"Not offhand, no. Once we get on the ground, Ginger, can you talk to her and see what you can find out?"

"Of course, Nik," the ginger cat, sitting beside Santa on the sleigh seat, agreed immediately. "I'm just glad all the, um, stuff, isn't getting into the sleigh."

"Speak for yourself," Santa told the cat with some asperity. "I've got brown spatters on my goggles, and it doesn't smell nice."

"Oh my," Ginger and Winky said at the same time.

"All right," Santa said, studying the heads-up display in his goggles, "I think that's Aniwa in the Vanuatu archipelago we're about to land on. I'm going to see about doctoring Prancer as best I can, then Berry can ride her back home to the vet."

"Santa, is that… one of the… volcanic islands?" Winky asked hesitantly, looking over his shoulder and gesturing; moments later, Berry's head popped up in the mouth of the bag.

"No. Well, it was once, but the volcano is extinct and gradually wore away as coral began to grow on it. Now it's kind of a sand bar on top of the coral reef. And it's inhabited—see the lights?" He pointed. "It'll be safe."

"It's very flat," Berry observed.

"Yes, because it basically is a really big sand bar," Santa agreed, easing the reindeer down to the deserted beach. "Which is good for us, because it isn't hard to land."

Moments later, the sleigh and team were on the ground, and Santa, Winky, and Berry climbed down from the sleigh, Ginger on Santa's shoulder. They walked over to Prancer, and Santa crouched down so Ginger could be eye to eye with the sick reindeer.

A series of trills, grunts, coughs, and hums ensued, as Ginger communicated with the animal. Finally Ginger turned to Santa.

"Well, this isn't good," Ginger said. "Someone fed her some of the egg nog."

"Oh no," Santa groaned. "No wonder she's so sick. Did any of the others get fed the egg nog?"

"No, she says not," Ginger said. "I asked that, right off, when I realized. But she's curious, and wondered what the 'two-legs' drink tasted like. She says it was good, but then it made her tummy burn and she burped a lot, then it turned into a lot more than that."

"As we saw," Santa said in dismay. "Well, let's see. Winky, will you go fetch the veterinary kit for me, and let's see if we can get her patched up enough to fly home."

"On it, Santa," Winky said, scampering for the regular stowage on the back of the sleigh.

By the time Santa and Winky were done treating Prancer, she was feeling well enough to fly home with Berry navigating, but Ginger ascertained that she wasn't up to pulling the sleigh any farther.

"Well, there's a reason why we fly with eight reindeer and not six," Santa noted. "I kind of wish it had been cloudy so I could have had nine, but his mate's expecting, and I could tell he wanted to be with her."

"Yeah, Rudy is the most like us of all the reindeer," Ginger agreed. "But we got this, Nik."

"I know. Let's get the rest of the harness off Prancer, then we'll see her and Berry off, and get in the air again, ourselves."

Santa had noted that Prancer's harness had suffered more damage in the flight, and he was concerned about Vixen and Blitzen, but everything went fine through Antarctica, Australia, and Asia. It wasn't until they were over Russia that things went really wrong.

They hit turbulence and there were a couple of sharp cracking sounds as the leather straps connecting Vixen's collar to the breast plate broke on one side; this meant the collar could drift upward and the breast plate fall down, causing the girth to loosen and potentially result in the harness coming completely loose from the sleigh's harness shaft.

And the sleigh was carrying a larger load than usual; kids had been very, very good that year. Six reindeer could probably manage to keep it aloft at this point, but Santa was worried; if the harness broke off suddenly, it could unbalance the team of deer and send the sleigh falling out of the sky.

It was obvious what had happened; the harness slid to one side on Vixen's body, and the consequences of a complete failure raced through Santa's mind in fractions of a second. Ginger felt his shoulder tense.

"Winky! Get up here! We've got an emergency!" Santa cried, and Winky all but jumped out of the bag. Santa pointed briefly with one hand; the off-center position of Vixen in the harness was pulling the sleigh to one side in its flight, and he fought it by adjusting the reins to counter the pull. "See that?"

"Oh, my goodness!"

"Can you get out there and fix it?"

"No, sir, I'm afraid I can't. I have the tools in here just in case, but I never studied under the leather workers."

"Mmph. Is there anyone on your Delivery team who has?"

"Let me go see."

"HURRY."

Winky was back moments later.

"No, sir. Major failing, but we were working with those who hadn't had the egg nog, so..." He shrugged in apology. "Can we land and have someone from the Pole do a rush delivery of a piece of leather?"

"Not here, nor anywhere close," Santa noted through gritted teeth as he fought the reins. "We're in the heart of Russia, and while the rural families still believe, the government is rather hostile these days. I had hopes for a while there, but then things... changed. Taking off and landing, other than for deliveries, isn't a good idea. And even the deliveries have to be... careful."

"Oh. Yes, I see. Um, we can pray? I have all the supplies to repair it, I think—if *you* know how to repair it..."

"I do, and good. But it isn't going to last until we can get somewhere safe to land, this time." He barked a rueful laugh. "It was easier to find a place to land over the Pacific than it will be, here." He shook his head. "Can you drive the team, then?"

"Yes, sir, I can do that!"

"Good. Get up here with the tool kit and take the reins from me. We'll have to do this on the fly—literally."

"Oh dear," Ginger murmured. "What can I do to help, Nik?"

"Stay here, safe in the sleigh, and pray," Santa replied, accepting the kit and handing over the reins to Winky.

Then he was up and over the front of the sleigh, straddling the sturdy tongue of the sleigh, before using the reindeer to pull himself along it.

It took a bit of doing, and the wind was fiercer outside the sleigh, but eventually Santa got to Vixen's place on the team. He reached out and grabbed the harness and pulled the deer closer to the tongue of the sleigh, then wrapped his legs tight around the tongue and used both hands to pull the broken leathers back together. Pulling a spool of heavy leather lacing from the kit in his front coat pocket, he bit off a length and began work, slowly stitching the broken leather straps back together. It wouldn't be the best repair job in the world, but it would hold for a while. He hoped that 'a while' would get them back to the Pole and home.

A hard, hurricane-like gust of wind nearly blew him off the sleigh tongue, but his legs were still wrapped tightly around it, and he was able to grab the more firmly-anchored pieces of Vixen's harness to pull himself back up to the top of the tongue. He decided immediately that the sense of hanging in open space, at least a mile up from the ground, was not a pleasant one. And the view of a reindeer's belly from down there wasn't much better.

Once the harness was pulled back together with the stitching, then tied off, Santa had to get himself back in the sleigh, which proved harder than getting out of it had been. He had to push and scoot backward and couldn't really see where he was going for the heavy coat and its fur collar.

"GINGER!" he cried. "Give me some direction, here!"

"Straight back, Nik, you're only about five feet out. Grab Comet's antlers, then push against it and the tongue and slide backward."

"I hope there aren't any splinters on this thing," Santa grumbled darkly. Ginger let out a cat laugh.

"So does Zara," he mumbled.

"I heard that. Shut up, kitty."

"Yes, sir!"

It took some time, but eventually Santa was back in the driver's seat in the sleigh, and a relieved Winky retired to the magick bag.

Ginger's tail was fluffed up bigger than Santa had ever seen it, but no one said anything about it.

"I never want to do that again," Santa declared. "Full tools with replacement leathers when we get home."

"Deal," Ginger agreed.

The rest of Europe had gone well; he'd made his stops in Africa—despite the population, there were fewer on that continent that celebrated Christmas, so it was sadly fairly quick—and across the Atlantic to South America. Then it was up through Central America, North America, and then home.

But in Guatemala, the land of volcanoes, there were several volcanoes erupting at that very time, and that meant earthquakes as well. It wasn't uncommon for this to happen, but it wasn't good that Santa had just taken a long drink from the thermos of hot chocolate laced with brandy. It seemed to rekindle the potency of the egg nog—which, after all, was not that long ago. Given Santa's ability to slow the flow of time, it had only been a couple of hours since Christmas Eve supper. And the nip of brandy in the cocoa meant that the quake that hit while he was in a home delivering gifts caused him to lose his balance.

The roar as the nearby Volcán Fuego erupted violently and simultaneously was disorienting enough.

The awkwardly-placed power cord for the Christmas tree was Santa's downfall, though.

He caught his toe on it and despite his best efforts, couldn't recover enough to stop the fall, though he staggered halfway across the room trying to retain his balance. The elf team spun in dismay as Santa landed on the floor with a hard thud and a loud grunt. The Christmas tree, yanked aside by the power cord, wobbled and commenced to topple.

"Oh no," Winky breathed.

Ginger leaped into action. He sailed through the outer branches of the artificial tree toward the nearby window, grabbing with all four paws as he went. His hind feet grabbed the metal tree trunk, while his front paws grabbed handfuls of window curtains. The curtains swung outward with the tension, but Ginger planned the maneuver well, and the tree, while tipped, did not fall. Then he hung on tightly until Santa could clamber back upright, regain his breath and his wits, and rescue the tree.

"Thanks, little fuzzball," he murmured. This was almost drowned out by the sound of cries from upstairs. "Oh bother, we woke the family. Or rather, I did. Let's go and go fast."

He waved his hand. A whirl of colors went around the room, then up the chimney...

...And there was no sign of gifts, Santa, elves, or a ginger cat.

They took care of delivering to neighboring houses while that family slowly settled and eventually went back to bed, all while watching the volcano's eruption with interest, curiosity, and a bit of concern. But it was far enough away from the village not to pose a threat, and the wind was blowing the ash away from them.

So in short order, and with greater care, Santa, Ginger, and Winky's team had the original house finished, and the sleigh took flight for the next village, making sure to stay away from Fuego.

"Finished!" Santa exclaimed in relief as they took care of the last house in Hawaii. "Now for home!"

"Finally," Ginger murmured. "That's a relief. We've had more things go wrong on this flight than in all the ones before, put together."

"Hush," Winky said, serious. "That's a good way to ensure we aren't done yet."

"Oh, quit being so superstitious!" Ginger grinned.

But Ginger thought better of it about halfway home.

They were still over the Pacific, cutting back across Alaska—to which they'd delivered toys after finishing the continental USA and Canada, on their way to Hawaii—when the repair job to Vixen's harness began to fail. Simultaneously, Blitzen's harness broke two leathers, and Dasher's harness started loosening.

"What gives?!" Santa exclaimed, trying to hold all the reindeer in position with the reins. "I didn't know Dasher's harness was even damaged!"

"With all the turbulence we've had, and the tugging and pulling the team did trying to avoid poor Prancer's vomit and, um, stuff, I'm not surprised," Ginger decided.

"I'm in agreement with Ginger," Winky agreed. "We probably need to just have the leather workers go over the whole thing when we get home."

"That's assuming we get home, at this rate," Santa grumbled. "Winky, take the reins; I'm going to try to do something I saw my father do once, and I need both hands."

"Got it," Winky said, accepting the reins and bracing himself inside the sleigh.

Santa stood—Ginger sank his front claws into the tail of his coat, then dug rear claws into the material of the seat, to help protect him from sudden gales—and closed his eyes, waving his hands in a pattern and mumbling something no one else could understand.

A streamer of rainbow light, rather like an aurora, poured from his hands and out to the reindeer. Wherever there was a broken piece of tack, rainbow light replaced it.

Santa swayed a bit as he opened his eyes, and Ginger quickly pulled him down and into the seat.

"There," Santa said. "That'll hold us a little while. Maybe until we get home, but maybe not. I know it won't last long. I'm tired and I don't have a lot of energy left to put into it. Please God, may it at least get us close."

It did let them get close. But not quite close enough. Santa's magickal time trick had already tired him, and now holding the harness together by what was mostly sheer willpower enhanced by that magick was tiring him even faster. He dropped the time magick, but that meant it took them longer to travel the distance home. Finally he was too tired to keep any of it up.

"All right, Winky, get your team out here," Santa told the elf. "I'm going to get you out of here."

"Huh? How?" Winky asked, as he summoned two more elves out of the gift bag.

"I'm going to put you each on one of the reindeer with the damaged harnesses, then cut them loose. With the lighter weight—no gifts, no elves, just one human—I should be able to get the sleigh back on half the team."

"Oh, you are NOT sending me away," Ginger complained, as the elves scurried about and got their equipment into their backpacks and prepared to depart the sleigh.

"It's for the best, Ginger," Santa told the cat earnestly. "I want to make sure you're safe. And the less weight, the better."

"I only weigh a few pounds and you know it. Who's going to make sure YOU are safe?"

"God."

"I never told you about what He told me, the mission He gave me when he gave us these gifts, did I?"

"No. Is there more to it than," Santa gestured around himself, "this?"

"Sort of, but not," Ginger said. "He told me, 'Ginger, he's going to need help. You're his helper.' And I said, but he's got Zara and Noam, what's left to do? And He said, 'Keep him safe. Make sure he knows when it's time to let go, when it's time to hang on, and when he's just being foolish. He's human, after all, and what I've given him won't stop him from making mistakes. But I've given you wisdom beyond your species, and you can be there for him in ways his wife and brother-in-law cannot.'"

Santa stared at him.

"All right," he finally conceded. "You can stay. Just... don't get either of us killed."

"I don't plan on it."

Fifteen minutes later, the elves were seated on the backs of Dasher, Vixen, and Blitzen, with hands holding tight to their antlers. In the sleigh behind them, Santa and Ginger sat ready.

"Ginger, you know what to tell 'em," Santa said, and Ginger let out a long, loud, warbling yowl.

All seven remaining reindeer shot to something approximating attention, then nodded. Dancer made a barking sound, and this was echoed by Dasher. Ginger turned to Santa.

"They know what to do, Nik," the cat said.

"All right. And... NOW!" Santa shouted, as he dropped the magicks.

Each elf pulled a Bowie knife and cut the traces holding their reindeer to the sleigh, and immediately the three deer broke formation with the others, leaping up, above the sleigh and away.

Meanwhile the other reindeer seemed to dig into invisible ground, hauling harder on the sleigh. It lurched twice, the first time downward, the second time, forward.

Exhausted, Santa simply hung onto the reins.

Ginger, whose rear claws were anchored in the seat cushions, held onto him.

Quickly the elves riding the reindeer disappeared ahead of the crippled sleigh, running ahead to warn the Arrival Team that Santa would be coming in fast and lacking in control, if he arrived at all, and to also prepare a search and rescue team if he didn't.

It was not a smooth ride back to the North Pole.

The polar vortex had spun up while they'd been gone, and the jet stream was roaring now. Four lone magickal reindeer had a hard time making headway toward their destination; the howling winds wanted to blow them off course. The turbulence was awful; the sleigh bucked and tossed, but it had been equipped with seat belts when those had come out in the human world for cars, and Santa had made sure to fasten himself securely. Ginger was also carefully harnessed to Santa's seat belt.

Santa simply held tight to the reins, his insulated gloves protecting his hands from the worst of the cold; without his having to ask, Ginger stretched up and pulled the neck gaiter out of the collar of Santa's coat, ensuring it went up and over his nose and ears.

"Thanks, little fuzzball," Santa responded. "That feels better. Get under my coattail and get warm."

So Ginger snuggled against Santa's side inside the big red coat; he heard Santa sigh.

"I run hotter than humans, huh?" he noted.

"Yes, and it feels awfully good right now."

"How close are we?"

"By my estimate we've got about another half an hour, forty-five minutes, if the reindeer can keep it up. Fighting the winds like this, I'm afraid they'll tire out before we get there."

"At least it's not snowing."

Just then, several flakes drifted past. Within seconds, it was a heavy flurry, obscuring the view ahead.

"You just had to say it, didn't you?" Santa grumbled.

There was an arrival runway just beside the castle, and Santa aimed for that.

But even magickal creatures and God-blessed humans have their limits.

The deer gave out just short of the runway, and came down in the evergreens that surrounded the castle.

The emergency team set off as soon as they saw the sleigh go down.

Zara bas Abram-Krisstoffsen, waiting beside the runway, screamed.

Nikolai Krisstoffsen, the one and only Santa Claus, gradually regained consciousness, realizing several things.

First, he ached all over. *Who beat me up?* he wondered. *And what did I do to deserve it?*

Second, he was warm. Comfortably so.

Third, there was a vibrating weight on his chest.

With a sigh, he opened his eyes, to see Zara bending over him with a smile, and Ginger in classic kitty loaf position on his chest, purring away. Only then did he realize he was home and in his own bed.

Memory came rushing back, and he tried to sit up, but Zara and Ginger managed to stop him.

"The team! The deer! The sleigh!" he exclaimed.

"Winky and his team came back on the deer you cut loose and told us what happened." Zara said softly. "They're fine. The deer that stayed harnessed to the sleigh are exhausted and being fed well and cared for. Vixen is over being fed spiked egg nog, and the sleigh is in the shop, getting the dents worked out. You're in pretty good shape, considering the landing. Nothing's broken, and while you were out of it for about a day, the doctor said it was more from exhaustion than a concussion or the like." She straightened. "You, my dear husband, are very, very lucky."

"Well, I did ask for help from Upstairs," Santa said. "Ginger? Did you make it okay?"

"A few bumps and bruises, but cats always land on their feet, Nik. You know that by now."

Santa chuckled, then grunted in pain.

Zara shook her head.

"And to think egg nog led to all this," she sighed. "No more rum, whiskey, bourbon, brandy or any other alcohol on Christmas Eve, I think. We can have it to celebrate after, but we almost didn't have an 'after' this time."

"I won't argue that," Santa decided. "Meanwhile, could I have some water, please?"

"That, I'll be happy to get," Zara said with a smile.

"...and so that's the reason Christmas Eve egg nog doesn't have alcohol in it anymore. Santa made it a rule after THAT Christmas!"

"Ohhhh, that explains why I can have it, then!"

"Exactly. He said if even he could get drunk by accident, they had no business putting alcohol in it on our busiest, most important night of the year."

"Ooo. Did anybody fuss?"

"No, they didn't. Everyone realized that flight was almost a disaster, and we could have lost the sleigh, the deer, the elves aboard, and Santa himself."

"Was Mrs. Claus upset?"

"She was upset about nearly losing Santa. But no, she decided to take it as a challenge, and come up with a terrific egg nog recipe that didn't NEED alcohol. I think she did great."

"I didn't think kitties could have egg nog. Not just th' alcohol, but th' spices."

"Well, I'm not an ordinary kitty, you know. I can have spices regular kitties can't. But I don't like alcohol—it makes me sneeze for ten solid minutes!—so Mrs. Claus always saved a mug for me before adding the alcohol." Ginger paused. "I think the no-alcohol recipes are better, personally. I like 'em better, anyway."

"Ohhhh. I get it."

"So, did you like the egg nog last Christmas?"

"Yes, it was good!"

"Good. Everyone agrees with you, so I think Mrs. Claus has finalized her recipe."

"Ha! And no more tripping an' knocking over Christmas trees for Santa?"

"Not a single time. Well, except for the time he had a bad head cold, about ten years ago. But he was so sick, he really shouldn't have been flying, and the family has been working on developing backup plans."

"Dat's good. So... he's speshul, but not, like, an angel?"

"He's a messenger, but he's what you might call a blessed human, I guess. Like how I'm a blessed cat. And you're not scared of me, are you?"

"No. You're soft and fluffy and purr-y."

Ginger laughed.

"In his own way, so is Santa," he said. "You just need to get to know him so you can see that. But you can't get to know him if you run away."

"Um... will you take me to him, so I can say I'm sorry?"

"Sure thing."

"...It's okay, Peanut," Santa said with a smile, as Almond hugged his son. "That happens more often than you might expect. I get word from my helpers who substitute for me at malls and events around the world that some human kids get scared, too."

"Dey do?"

"They do, yes. Oh! I have an idea."

"What?" Peanut asked

"If I put together a team to brainstorm how to fix that, would you be interested in helping me by being on the team and giving me advice? Maybe along with your dad?"

Peanut's eyes grew wide, and he cast a glance at his father at the same time Almond looked at him. The adult elf raised an eyebrow and nodded at his son. Peanut beamed.

"YES sir!" he exclaimed. "I want to help!"

"Very good!" Santa said with a smile. "Let me talk to some of the others, and we'll put together a team to come up with ideas for how to make Santa less scary for shy children, and I'd really like you to head it, Peanut."

"Me?!"

"Yes. How better to know what would work than by having someone who understands what it's like? Your dad can help you wherever you have problems or aren't sure, and I'm always available to talk to about it."

Peanut considered for a long moment, and the others waited. Finally he looked up.

"I will do my bestest, Santa," the young one said very seriously.

"Very good, then," a pleased Santa said, as Ginger leaped back to his shoulder. "We'll get out of your way, then, and let you get back to work, Almond."

"Thank you, Santa," Almond said, a grateful look in his eyes.

"Don't thank me, thank Ginger, here. I don't know what he told Peanut, but it seems to have worked."

Ginger grinned, then held his paw up to his mouth, letting one toe rest against his lips as he looked at Peanut.

"I won't tell!" Peanut responded, and giggled.

"Hmm," Santa said, raising an eyebrow, then turning away from a grinning Almond and a giggling Peanut. "Just between the two of you, eh?"

"Of course," Ginger said, grinning wider. "Though I just might tell that team Peanut is going to run."

"But not me."

"Nope."

"Zara?"

"Maybe."

"You always were hard to understand. And into mischief."

"Always out of love, Nik. Always."

"Yeah. I love you, too, little fuzzball. I love you, too."

If you enjoyed this short story and want more of Ginger, Nik/Santa, and their family, you can learn about their origins in The Gingerbread Cat, *a novella by Stephanie Osborn.*

Tattered Angel

By Dale Kesterson

It was the day before Christmas. Evelyn Weldon leaned back in the cab with a sigh and glanced at her granddaughter beside her. Andrea was quiet, which was unusual. The usual bright, bubbling enthusiasm remained absent. More telling, she had asked no questions. They were on their way to the hospital to visit Andrea's mother Deidra.

Andrea held a box on her lap. No amount of persuasion could convince Andrea to leave the shoebox with shabby-looking torn corners at home. Andrea claimed it was a special present for her mother for Christmas and insisted on bringing it with them. She wouldn't say what it was, or let Evelyn look inside the box. Evelyn gave up after five minutes of discussion—her granddaughter had inherited her own determination.

At their destination, while Andrea gazed at the decorations in the busy lobby, Evelyn exchanged nods with the hospital receptionist. Although the visitation rules stated no children under the age of twelve were allowed to see patients, she had asked permission to bring Andrea in to see her mother. Deidra had been in a car accident. Following surgery for multiple injuries complications had set in, and she was admitted to the intensive care unit for five days. Evelyn spent those long days in the ICU waiting room, seeing her daughter for five minutes every hour, until last night when Deidra was moved to a private room. She was far from well, and Andrea had special permission to visit her mother.

"We'll take the elevator to the fifth floor," Evelyn explained to Andrea. "Once we get to your mother's room, we won't stay long. The weather report said it's going to snow and I want to be home before it gets too messy outside."

She saw Andrea nod her agreement, the box clutched to her chest.

Once out of the elevator, Evelyn guided the youngster down the hall. The rounded counter of the hospital nurses' station was decorated with silk garlands of evergreens, holly, and poinsettias. Evelyn had a firm hold on Andrea's hand as they walked up to it.

"Good morning, Mrs. Weldon," the nurse on duty greeted her. "This must be Andrea."

"Good morning, Miss Smitherman," Evelyn replied with a smile. "Yes, this is Deidra's daughter, Andrea."

"Forgive me for saying this, but you told me she's almost eleven. She doesn't look that old."

"She's small for her age, but bright. She'll be eleven at midnight."

"A Christmas baby! How lucky for her."

Evelyn briefly glanced down at her only grandchild. There was more to Andrea's birth than being a Christmas baby, but she didn't want to go into details. "Andrea and her mother are very close. I appreciate you bending the rules for her."

"We can make exceptions, especially for the holidays. We try to discharge anyone we can, and relax the rules for anyone who has to stay." Miss Smitherman smiled at Andrea. "I see you've brought something with you, Andrea."

Andrea smiled up at the nurse. "It's a Christmas present for my mother."

"The present is in your box?" asked the nurse.

"Uh-huh. It's something very special, a doll. I know Momma will love it."

"Andrea," began Miss Smitherman as she came around the counter, "you know your mother is very sick." As Andrea nodded, the nurse knelt and gently said, "I need to see what's in the box to make sure it's not something which will make her worse. You're old enough to understand."

"I understand, but it won't hurt her." Andrea hesitated, then removed the cover.

The nurse saw a soiled, cloth doll with a ragged dress, faded painted face, and straggly brown yarn hair lying in a nest of crumpled Christmas wrapping paper.

Evelyn peered over the nurse's shoulder and gasped. It was Andrea's old doll, and she had dragged it around everywhere she went for ten years. Although she saw Andrea had tried to wash the small muslin figure, the doll was as shabby as the box she lay in.

"I'm sorry, Andrea," said Miss Smitherman, looking into the girl's face with compassion, "but I can't let you take this into your mother's room. Your doll is too dirty to be good for your mother—we have to keep everything clean in her room. You can visit your mother, but the doll will have to stay out here with me."

Evelyn saw tears in her granddaughter's eyes, which Andrea quickly wiped away as she put the top back on the shoebox. She knew how much this visit meant to the child, and she also knew giving the doll away was a sacrifice for Andrea. She sighed, her heart aching.

An aide came up to Miss Smitherman. "I gave Mrs. Milton her bath. It tired her out and she's taking a nap."

"Thank you, Gwen." Miss Smitherman turned to Evelyn. "I don't think she should be disturbed right now. You're welcome to wait in the lounge. I'll come down when she wakes up."

"Come on, Andrea. We can figure out another gift for your mother while we wait." Evelyn took Andrea's hand and they walked down the hallway to the visitor's lounge.

Once seated, Evelyn turned to her grandchild. "Honey, I know you want to give your mom something special, but that's your favorite doll. You take it everywhere. Are you sure you want to give it away?" She hoped this would be less painful than pointing out the nurse was right about the doll's condition.

"That's why it's special," Andrea mumbled, her eyes still teary. "Grandma, I tried to clean her up by giving her a bath."

"That was a good idea." Evelyn paused as she sought a way to help the distressed girl. She rubbed her forehead with her fingers as she tried to think. She was tired, and the strain of having to divide her time between her daughter and her granddaughter over the past week had taken a toll on her emotions. The idea that Andrea was willing to give up the doll, which she slept with every night, had deeply touched her. "Tell you what. Let's see if we can shop for a special present for your mom."

"Would you let me go shopping by myself?" Andrea asked. "That way you can stay here in case Momma wakes up from her nap."

"Do you think you can?" replied Evelyn. She knew her granddaughter was mature for her age, independent-minded, and responsible.

"Yes, Grandma." Andrea's voice was firm.

Evelyn held a fast debate in her mind. "All right, I'll trust you to be careful. I'll wait here to see your mother, while you go shopping." She reached into her purse. "Do you have your wallet in your bag?" she asked, referring to the small shoulder purse Andrea carried everywhere.

"Uh-huh." Andrea dug it out.

"Here, take this ten-dollar bill. There are a few gift shops within a couple of blocks from here. You don't have to get anything big or expensive. Your mother will love whatever you give her because it's from you."

Andrea nodded, her face solemn. "I understand, Grandma."

"Don't go too far and come back as soon as you can. I don't want you to stay out longer than two hours. It will be lunchtime by then and we can eat in the cafeteria."

Andrea put her wallet back in her bag, and looked at her watch. "I'll be back before one o'clock," she promised as she gave Evelyn a hug. "I love you."

"I love you, too." Evelyn watched as Andrea made her way down the hall to the elevator.

Andrea took the elevator down to the first floor. She trudged to the main entrance to the hospital and looked out of the glass doors. She knew it was cold outside, and the snowfall had started, making the morning darker.

"Christmas Eve snow," she thought to herself. "It has a magic of its own. Maybe it will let me find a way to help Momma."

She crossed to one of the lobby chairs and carefully placed the shoebox on it. She zipped up her jacket, and wound her scarf around her head and neck. She then pulled her gloves out of her pockets and put them on before she picked the box up again. Andrea cradled it like she would a baby and peeked inside. She saw her doll as a treasure, not something dirty and worn.

"I don't care what the nurse says," she whispered to her doll. "I love you and Mommy does too. I know you'll help her get better. I just have to figure out some way to get you fixed up." She closed it and hugged the box to her chest while she leaned on the door and stepped out into the cold.

The north wind bit into her face as Andrea went down the steps. When she reached the sidewalk, she looked both ways, trying to decide where to start. She had two hours, and knew exactly what she wanted, but was unsure of how to get it.

"I'm almost eleven now," she murmured to herself, "and I can take care of myself. The stores are open. I need special help, and it's Christmas Eve. It's magic." She checked to make sure her little purse was snapped closed. Inside it, the ten-dollar bill was secure in her wallet. "If I'm late, I'll tell Grandma I lost track of time looking for something." With a firm nod of determination, she set off down the sidewalk toward the nearest stores.

The first one she came to had lots of pretty figurines in the window, all set out on decorated boxes among ribbons and little trees.

"Maybe someone in here will know how to help me," she thought.

A woman coming out held the door for her as she ducked into the warmth of the shop.

"Thank you," Andrea politely told her.

"Merry Christmas," the lady replied as she went on her way.

"You, too."

Andrea walked around for a minute before she found the display of wrapping paper and ribbons.

"May I help you?" a woman wearing a shop smock asked, smiling down at her.

Andrea looked at the ribbons and bows. "Those are nice. Are they expensive?"

"Do you want a ribbon to tie around your box?" The saleslady regarded the slightly grubby shoebox.

"No, I want—" She hesitated. "My mother is in the hospital and I want to give her something special for Christmas."

The woman's face softened. "I'm sorry your mother is in the hospital. I'll try to help you find the perfect gift. Do you think she would like a sweet little ceramic angel? We have some lovely ones. Why don't we look at them?"

The saleslady led her over to a glass case. Inside it were angel figurines of different sizes, with sparkling wings and golden halos. Some held little harps, others held Christmas wreaths, and one had a dove perched on her hand. Andrea studied them and saw the price tag on the smallest one was twenty-five dollars. She turned to face the woman.

"Those are beautiful, and I'm sure my mother would love one, but I only have ten dollars." She hoped she sounded braver than she felt.

"I'm sorry, all the angels are more than that. Why did you ask about the ribbons?"

"I want to give my mother my doll, but the nurse won't let me. I thought if I could make her look nice—" Andrea stopped again. "I mean, I need to find a way to make my doll pretty enough to give her as a present."

"I'm afraid I don't understand, dear," the lady said, bending over. "You have a doll?"

"Here in my box." Andrea took one glove off, stuffed it in her pocket, and carefully removed the top of the shoebox. "She's my favorite. See?"

The lady peered into the box. "Oh, surely you don't want to give this doll as a Christmas present," the woman gently chided as her forehead creased with a frown. "It's old and dirty. I'm afraid a ribbon won't help. Let's see if I can help you find a nicer gift. We have other things for sale. How about a small snow globe? You know, the kind you shake to make the snow inside it swirl around the scene? I can show you one with an angel in it and it would cost you ten dollars."

Andrea knew the woman meant well. "Thank you, but I have to get going." She put the cover back on the box, and pulled on her glove. "Merry Christmas." She left.

Back out on the street, she noticed the snow was coming down harder and starting to stick to the pavement. She walked down the block and stopped in front of another gift shop.

The window display had dolls, some dainty and small. All of them had nice clothes.

"This looks more promising than the first one," she thought. Smiling, she pushed the door open and went in.

The store was large, with a counter along the side, close to the front door.

"Hello," she said to the woman behind the counter. "Do you sell doll clothes?"

"I'm afraid we don't have separate clothes for dolls. We only sell the dolls you see here. Are you looking for something specific?"

"I have a doll, but she needs a new dress." Andrea, remembering the reaction of the first saleslady, bit her lip, not sure how she should explain it. "She's special to me, and I want to give her as a gift, but she's a little dirty and needs to look nicer."

"Is your doll in the box?"

"Yes, ma'am." Andrea took the cover off her shoebox. "I know she's not very pretty now, but I was hoping with a new dress, she'd be pretty enough to give away."

"I'm not sure a new dress would help much," the woman said, not unkindly. "You say you want to give her away as a gift?"

Andrea nodded. "My mother is in the hospital. She knows how special my doll is to me and I want her to have it." She felt tears filling her eyes and looked down at the floor for a moment to hide them.

"It's your doll?"

"It's my favorite," Andrea explained. "I've had it as long as I can remember."

"What's your name?"

"Andrea."

"I'm really sorry, Andrea, but I don't have anything which would help you with your doll. Would you like to look at some new ones? Perhaps you can find one she'd like."

The woman came out from behind the counter, and showed her some nice cloth dolls that might have been like hers when it was new. When Andrea saw the price tags, though, she knew she couldn't afford one, even if she found the right doll.

"You've been very nice to me," said Andrea to the woman, "but I only have ten dollars to spend. I guess I'll keep looking."

"Andrea, I hope your mother gets better," the woman said. "Maybe Christmas will bring you good luck."

"Thank you," Andrea replied as she pulled on her gloves. She sniffed back a few more tears. "Merry Christmas."

"It's Christmas Eve, and it's snowing. I have to believe there's Christmas magic!" she thought to herself. "Christmas has a magic of its own," she murmured out loud as she stepped into the fluffy flakes falling from the sky.

The snow was over an inch deep on the sidewalk. Andrea knew her grandmother would be worried about her, and almost started back to the hospital, but as she turned around, she saw a small shop she hadn't noticed before, directly opposite where she stood, across the street. There wasn't much traffic on the street, but she went to the corner, patiently waited for the light to change before crossing, and walked the short distance back to shop.

This store was dingier than the others. An old metal sign over the doorway had one word on it: GIFTS. The sign in the window said it was open, but although she could see toys on display, the window was dark. Andrea hesitated for a moment.

"This is my last chance," she thought. "The snow is getting thicker, and I'm running out of time. It's either go in and see if they have anything, or go back to the hospital now." She frowned. "Well, I can't go back without a present." She decided to give the shop a try.

Andrea took a deep breath, and grasped the old-fashioned handle which had a latch instead of a knob. As the door opened, some bells over her head jangled as the top of it hit them. The inside of the shop was a little gloomy, yet somehow it didn't seem scary.

"Hello?" she said in a loud voice, a bit uncertain. "The sign said the shop is open."

"Come in, come in! Welcome! Merry Christmas!" a man's voice called out. "Wait—I'm in the back, changing a fuse, and then I'll turn on the lights. I'm almost done."

Andrea heard a noise which sounded like a metal cabinet shutting.

"There! Let's see if that does it," the man's voice added.

Suddenly, the shop was filled with all kinds of lights! Andrea squealed with delight. There were decorated trees with strings of Christmas lights, and a beautiful carousel with lights, sitting on a round table, started to turn. She saw baby dolls, dolls with cloth bodies and porcelain faces and hands, and dolls dressed in outfits from other countries, all in glass showcases. In another corner, she saw toy trains set up on tables and three rocking horses. The shop was a child's dream of toy land!

"Now, young lady, what may I do for you?" A small man with a fringe of white hair around his head, a white beard, and wearing wire-rimmed glasses that hung on the end of his nose, came toward her. He wiped his hands on a towel. His face was wrinkled and his blue eyes were kind and friendly. He wore a shop apron, and she could see some tools poking out of its pockets.

"I hope you can help me," she began. "My mother is in the hospital and I want to give her my favorite doll, but everyone says she's too old and too dirty."

"How long have you had your doll?"

"When I was little, my father told me he gave it to me. When I was older, my mother told me that he gave it to me the night I was born. He's gone to heaven," she replied. Her eyes filled with tears, and her words came out in a rush. "Now my mother is very sick. I can't stay with her, so I want to give her my doll so she'll know I love her. I know it will help my mother get better. I love my doll—she's special because my father gave her to me."

"She is a special doll, indeed," the man agreed. "Have you taken good care of her?"

Andrea's face flushed with embarrassment, but she forced herself to meet his eyes. "I've tried. When I was little, I used to take her everywhere with me, but her dress got torn and she's not pretty anymore." She took a breath. "I don't care about that. I tried to give her a bath yesterday, but it didn't help." The shop was warm, so she took off her gloves, unwound her scarf, and unzipped her jacket.

"Does she have a name?"

"Angel." A tear made its way down her cheek. "I'm sorry. I don't mean to cry but I'm really worried about my mother."

"My name is Chris. What's yours?"

"Andrea. Andrea Milton."

"You said your mother is in the hospital?"

"Yes, she was in a bad car accident, she had surgery, and she's very sick. She was in intensive care, but now she's in her own room." Andrea wiped her tears away with the back of her hand.

"I heard about the accident, and I know you're scared," Chris told her, his voice warm and gentle. "Andrea, may I see your doll?"

Andrea felt she could trust him to look at the doll without wincing the way everyone else had. She gave him the box and watched as he opened it.

Chris gazed down at the little cloth doll before looking up at Andrea. She tried to look calmer than she felt. At least he wasn't telling her how dirty Angel was.

"May I pick her up?" he asked.

"Do you think you can fix her so I can give her to my mother?"

"I don't want to promise anything before I know for sure, but I've been making dolls for a long time."

"Do what you can," Andrea felt a glimmer of hope for the first time. "Oh, please! Angel means a lot to me."

With great care, Chris lifted the worn figure from its nest of paper and examined it from all sides, gently turning it over. "Andrea, who named the doll Angel?"

"I think my father did when he gave it to me. Is that important?"

"In a way. I think I know why he did." Chris regarded her with a smile. "How old is she?"

"She's as old as I am. I'll be eleven tonight."

"Tonight?" He looked thoughtful.

"According to my mother, I was born at midnight." Andrea decided to tell him the story. "Momma says my head was born right before midnight and the rest of me was born right after it. My mother calls me her Christmas miracle."

"That makes you as special as your doll."

"Now that I'm old enough, I get to stay up until midnight on Christmas Eve," she proudly confided. She bit her lip and lowered her gaze to the cloth doll. "What do you think? Can you fix her?"

"Andrea, did you know your doll is an angel?" He smiled down at the doll, then looked up at her. "I guess we could say that now she's a tattered angel."

"She is? I mean, I know she's dirty and her dress is torn, but she's an angel?" Surprised, Andrea studied the doll she took to bed every night.

"Oh, yes, definitely. See these places on her back?" Chris turned the doll face down. "Her wings used to be here." He showed her two seams with uneven stitches on the doll's dress. "And this," he continued, pointing to the back of her head, "is where her halo was."

"I don't remember her having wings or a halo," murmured Andrea, frowning while she thought about it.

"I think perhaps your father gave you Angel to watch over you and keep you safe. Over the years, her wings were damaged, so someone took them off and sewed up where they went." Chris smiled at her and his eyes twinkled.

Andrea smiled back. "Can you mend her?"

"I believe I can," he answered.

"Oh, thank you!" Relief flooded her voice and she started to relax, then recalled two problems. She cleared her throat and swallowed hard. "Uh, Mr. Chris? Before you start, I have to be back in the hospital by one o'clock to have lunch with my grandmother. How long will it take—I mean, if you can do it?"

"I have my sewing machine and other things in my workroom, so this shouldn't take long," he assured her.

"The other thing I need to know is, how expensive is it going to be? My grandmother gave me ten dollars to buy a gift for my mother. Would you be able to fix her for that?" Andrea's voice became wistful as she dug into her bag and pulled out her wallet. She took out the ten, along with a one-dollar bill. "I'd love to get her a new dress, too. Would that cost more? There's a dollar of my own to add to the ten, but that's all I have." Her voice shook a little as she fought back more tears. "I know it should probably be more, but will this be enough? I wouldn't want you to start working on Angel and then not be able to pay you for it."

Chris studied her for a long moment before he said anything. Andrea watched his eyes closely, almost afraid to hope he'd say yes. Anxious, she held her breath and waited.

"Well, now," Chris said, stroking his beard, "I think the repairs would be exactly ten dollars, and your extra dollar will be enough for a new dress."

Andrea breathed a sigh of relief. "Please, Mr. Chris, make her pretty again."

"What's your mother's favorite color?" he asked.

She didn't have to think hard about that and grinned. "That's easy! Pink."

"There's a chair next to the carousel. It has a switch on it to play music. Give me fifteen minutes."

"Don't you want my money?" she asked, holding it out to him.

"Keep it until I'm finished." Humming a song which sounded familiar, Chris disappeared into the back room of his shop.

Andrea was too wound up to sit still for fifteen minutes, but she found the switch Chris mentioned. Sounds of Christmas carols filled the shop, and she wandered around, admiring all the amazing toys. She kept looking at her watch as the fifteen minutes dragged on.

Finally, Chris reappeared, with a broad smile on his face. His eyes twinkled merrily as he laid a sparkly sheet of tissue paper on the counter, and placed an angel doll on it.

"Andrea, here's Angel."

Andrea could not believe her eyes. The doll's newly-painted face was serene, her wings were quilted, her hair was done in a bun, her halo was a golden wire, and her dress was pink with white lace. She looked brand new.

"That's my doll?" she asked, her voice shaky. Tears tumbled out of her eyes and flowed down her cheeks. She wiped them with the sleeve of her jacket.

"Yes, Andrea, that's your Angel." Chris chuckled as he reached down under the counter and pulled out a new box. "Go ahead, pick her up."

With trembling hands, Andrea picked up her favorite doll. "She's beautiful!" A long-lost memory came back to her. "This is what she used to look like!" She looked up at the man with the dancing blue eyes and handed Angel back to him. "How did you do it?"

"You loved Angel with all the love only a child can give to a doll," he explained as he wrapped the doll in the tissue paper. Once Angel was in her new box, he closed it, tied a beautiful pink ribbon around it, and made a wonderful bow. "I brought some of that love out of her and used it to help make her better." He put the box into a plain, brown paper shopping bag, and reached under the counter again. This time he offered her a box of tissues. "Would you like to blow your nose?"

"Thank you." Andrea pulled a tissue from the box and used it, then dropped it in a waste basket. Smiling once again, she handed him the eleven dollars. "Are you sure this is enough? I think I can get more from my grandmother and bring it back here."

Chris took the money. "Andrea, eleven dollars is the perfect amount—one dollar for every year of the love you gave to Angel."

"How can I thank you?" She picked up the bag.

"Give Angel to your mother, and keep believing in Christmas miracles," he said with a sad sort of smile. "Now, you need to get back to the hospital. It's already after twelve, and the snow is getting deeper."

Chris came around the counter, and held the bag with the precious gift while she zipped her jacket, put on her scarf, and pulled on her gloves.

Shyly, she stared into the merry blue eyes behind his glasses. "Thank you, Mr. Chris." She took the box, hesitated, and then hugged him. "Oh, thank you so much!"

"Ah, that's my tip," he said with a chuckle. "You're welcome." He opened the door, and reached up to turn the OPEN sign to CLOSED.

"You're closing?"

"I won't get any more customers today, the weather is too bad." He sighed and Andrea saw his eyes tear up. "Christmas Eve can be odd, even strange sometimes. I remember one, a few years ago, when I stayed open past midnight. Good thing I did, too. I had one last customer who needed a special present."

"Like I did today?"

"Yes, like you did." Chris pulled a handkerchief out of his pocket and blew his nose. "That's enough of my memories. You be careful walking back to the hospital. The sidewalks are slippery."

She stepped outside and waved to him as he closed the door, humming the same song she heard earlier.

The sky was grey, the snowflakes were smaller, and what was on the sidewalk was deeper. She went back to the corner, crossed the street, and started back to the hospital. She glanced at the toy shop as she passed it. The lights were out, and it looked dingy again.

"Well, Mr. Chris did say he was closing up," she said to herself.

She concentrated on walking. The sidewalk was slippery now, and Andrea knew she had to go slowly. Andrea was on the steps of the hospital when she realized the song Chris hummed was, "Santa Claus is Coming to Town." She laughed out loud.

In the elevator on the way back up to the fifth floor, Andrea made a decision.

"Mr. Chris tied the bow around the box so I can't show Angel to Grandma. I'm going to surprise her, too. I won't tell her what happened. I'll wait until Momma opens the box," she said to herself.

She took the elevator up to the fifth floor and found her grandmother in the lounge.

"Thank heavens you're back," Evelyn greeted her. "I was getting worried. The snow is coming down harder and I heard a weather report. It's going to get worse."

"I was careful walking," Andrea replied. "It's a bit slippery, though." She held up the shopping bag.

"You found a gift for your mother?" Evelyn tried to hide her surprise. "For ten dollars?"

"Uh-huh. Well, really, it was eleven dollars. I used the money you gave me, and I had a dollar of my own from my allowance," replied Andrea with a grin. "Momma is going to love it."

"What did you get her?"

"Grandma, I'd like you to wait until I give it to her. Would you mind? I promise, it's something wonderful," Andrea said with a bashful smile.

"I suppose so," Evelyn agreed. "Is it wrapped?"

Andrea lifted the box out of the shopping bag. "Sort of. The shop owner tied a ribbon around it."

"What a lovely bow! She did a good job with the ribbon." Privately, Evelyn was relieved to see it was a new box, although she could not imagine what was inside. She knew ten dollars was not a lot of money, especially at Christmas.

"It was a Mister, not a Miss," Andrea informed her. "I was lucky to find his shop. The owner was great."

"Where is it?" Evelyn asked.

Before Andrea could respond, Miss Smitherman entered the lounge.

"Oh, I'm glad to see you're back, Andrea—and you have a new gift! That's wonderful. Mrs. Welton, your daughter is awake. I told her that Andrea is here."

"How is she, Miss Smitherman?" Evelyn fought down the fears that crowded her mind. Her daughter had been through terrible ordeals in the past eleven years, and had always been delicate.

"She's still in serious condition, but she's improving. She's looking forward to seeing Andrea. Are you ready?"

Evelyn gathered up their coats and Andrea put her gift back in the shopping bag. They followed the nurse down the hall. Evelyn thought she heard her granddaughter softly humming "Santa Claus Is Coming To Town" as they approached Deidra's room.

"At least she's happier than she was this morning," Evelyn thought to herself with relief. She knew this visit would do them all good.

"Wait here until I call you in," Miss Smitherman requested. She knocked on the closed door, and entered after a short pause.

"Deidra, you have a couple of visitors, if you're ready," she said as she pulled the door shut behind her.

Less than a minute later, the nurse ushered them in.

Evelyn took Andrea's hand and led her to the side of hospital bed. "Ignore the IV line, the traction cords and pulleys."

Deidra smiled at her daughter. "Hello, my dearest sweetheart."

"Momma?" Andrea turned to the nurse. "Miss Smitherman, may I hug her?" She handed the shopping bag to her grandmother.

"If you do it gently," the nurse cautioned.

Evelyn and the nurse watched as the small girl awkwardly reached around the medical equipment to give her mother a hug and a kiss on the cheek.

"Momma, I love you," Andrea murmured. "I've been so worried and I couldn't come to see you. Please, get better."

"I love you, too, my dearest," Deidra replied. "Just seeing you helps."

"I'm going back out to the desk, Mrs. Welton," the nurse told Evelyn. "Use the call button if you need anything."

"Miss Smitherman? I'd like you to stay a moment, if you can," said Andrea, to Evelyn's surprise. "I know you were concerned about my gift and I'd like you to see it for yourself."

"Of course, if you want me to," the nurse replied. "I'd love to see your mother's present."

"Thank you." Andrea turned back to her mother. "Momma, I have a Christmas present for you."

Evelyn stepped forward to hold the bag for her granddaughter. She watched as Andrea took the box out of the shopping bag and stood holding it with a shy smile on her face.

"Momma, I wish I could stay here with you all the time, but I know I can't. I thought about it and I want you to have a special gift of love that you can keep with you." Andrea extended the present to her mother. "Merry Christmas."

"It's a beautiful ribbon," Deidra said. She managed to get the ribbon off the box with the bow intact. "Maybe Miss Smitherman can find somewhere to hang it." She put the bow aside. "Andrea, would you help me open the box?"

Together, the two got the cover off. Evelyn and the nurse moved closer to the bed to see the gift. Deidra carefully peeled back the sparkly tissue paper and gasped.

"Angel!" Deidra whispered the name. Slowly, she lifted the angel doll out of her wrappings. "Mother, look! It's Angel!" Her voice cracked with emotion. "She looks exactly the way she did when David first gave her to Andrea!"

Evelyn felt her eyes fill with tears.

"What a beautiful angel doll!" exclaimed Miss Smitherman. "Andrea, where did you find it?"

Deidra reached one hand out to her daughter while she held the doll with her other arm. "Dearest, how did you get this?"

"I wanted to give you something I love, so it could love you and keep you company when I'm not here," Andrea explained. "I chose Angel. I hope I put enough love into her so she could love you just as much. She can do that when I can't be with you, and help you get better."

"Andrea, is this the same doll you brought with us this morning?" Evelyn asked, her voice full of wonder. "I thought you were going to shop for something new."

"I didn't have to. I found a kind old man in a small shop and he fixed her. He told me I gave her so much love that he used some of it to mend her and make her pretty again." Andrea put her hand on her mother's hand, the one holding Angel. "You do love her, don't you?"

"Yes, my dearest. I love her and I love you." Deidra paused to wipe tears off her face. "I told you that your father gave Angel to you when you were a baby. He loved you, and thought she would watch over you." Smiling, she nodded to Evelyn. "Right?"

"Yes, I remember," Evelyn agreed. She dug into her purse for a tissue and dabbed her eyes. She turned to the nurse, who stood with an expression of disbelief. "Andrea's birth was difficult and we almost lost her. David, her father, bought the angel doll for her that snowy Christmas Eve night and put it by her crib. She's taken it to bed every night ever since."

"You mean this is the same doll I saw this morning?" Miss Smitherman asked. She folded her arms over her chest. "That's impossible. It would have taken a miracle."

"A Christmas Eve miracle. Like my baby daughter." Deidra smiled at Andrea. "It's almost as if your father was here, too."

"Momma, I hope Angel will help you get better," Andrea whispered, so softly Evelyn could barely hear it.

"You couldn't have given me a better gift, my dearest," Deidra murmured in response. "She will remind me of all the love we shared, especially when you were born."

A moment of silence fell over the room.

"I hear sirens," Evelyn commented. "Not here, but a little farther away, from the sounds."

Gwen, the aide, knocked on the door. "Excuse me for interrupting. Miss Smitherman? The sirens aren't ambulances—they're fire trucks. A fire just broke out in a building down the street!"

"Which one?"

"That small abandoned building right across the street from the gift shop that sells those lovely dolls." Gwen shivered. "It's a good thing no one has been in that old store for years."

"Is that the one that had a metal sign over the door?" Andrea asked. "The sign with one word. Gifts."

Gwen nodded.

Evelyn noticed Andrea's face looked thoughtful. "Did you see the shop when you were out shopping, Andrea?" she asked.

"Uh-huh, I did," Andrea admitted. "It's funny, too. I thought I saw someone there."

"That's the building," Miss Smitherman agreed. "But Andrea, you couldn't have seen anyone there. The shop owner died eleven years ago, on Christmas Day. He collapsed in his workroom, the police found him, and brought him here to the emergency room." She sighed. "We couldn't help him." The nurse paused for a moment, then smiled. "I haven't thought about him for years. I remember he had a real knack for making wonderful toys. His name was Chris. We used to call him Chris Cringle, because he reminded us of Santa Claus."

"What did he look like?" Deidra asked the nurse.

"He was a small, old man, almost bald with a fringe of white hair around his head," the nurse replied. "What I remember the most were his eyes. They were blue and merry."

"I remember him now!" Gwen exclaimed. "Didn't he wear wire-rimmed glasses?"

"Yes, and they always looked like they were about to fall off the end of his nose, but they never did," Miss Smitherman added with a chuckle. "He was a generous man, always making small gifts for kids, especially at Christmastime. What was really funny was he always hummed the same song as he worked."

"Momma, I bet I know what it was," said Andrea to her mother.

Evelyn exchanged glances with her daughter, and they both turned to look at Andrea.

"What was the song?" Deidra asked.

"Santa Claus Is Coming To Town." Andrea stood next to the bed, a big grin on her face. "He was kind and gentle," she told her mother.

"How do you know?" the nurse asked. "He died the night you were born."

Evelyn thought Andrea was going to argue, but saw her looking thoughtful again.

"Andrea?" she prompted.

"Miss Smitherman, you should believe in Christmas miracles," Andrea told her. She reached out to Evelyn, who moved toward the bed.

"Like a tattered doll turning into a beautiful angel?" Evelyn said with a knowing smile as she took Andrea's hand.

"Yes, Grandma. A time when love can take a tattered angel and make it beautiful again." Andrea beamed.

"Like a beautiful baby girl who survived," Deidra added, looking at Andrea with brimming eyes. "After all, it's Christmas Eve, and it is snowing."

Author Biographies

<u>Jordan Campbell</u> was born in Santa Cruz, California and moved to Maine when he was eleven years old. Always eager to read anything he could get his hands on, Jordan is excited at the opportunity to bring his own stories to the world.

Anna and Tod Casasent together write as <u>A. Kristina Casasent</u>. They serve the whims of their Newfoundland dog, Mini American Shepherd dog, Maine Coon cat, calico cat, and Crested Gecko. Living in Texas, the couple does science by day and writes fiction by night. Their weekly blog is found at <u>https://blog.casasent.blog</u>.

<u>Eppie Gray</u> is the pen name for Tiffanie Gray in the children's story genre. Tiffanie was a teacher for 25 years in all different grade levels and loves writing stories with good values and interesting worlds that entice young listeners and readers and still touch an adult's fancy. Eppie's Fuzzy Friends Learning books can currently be found on Amazon.

<u>Lydia Sherrer</u> is the award-winning and USA Today Bestselling author of the *Love, Lies, and Hocus Pocus Universe* of books which have sold nearly a million copies worldwide. Most recently she has published a *Gamelit* series, *Trans Dimensional Hunter*, with NYT bestselling author John Ringo, and has written stories for several *Black Tide Rising* anthologies.

<u>Aaron Canton</u> is an author who specializes in YA fantasy stories as well as having written content for RPGs and other games. His work has been published in the *Fantastic Schools* anthology series, the Raconteur Press anthology *Corsairs and Cutlasses*, and *Phobos Magazine*. He lives in Salt Lake City, Utah.

Fran Van Cleave has written for 'Analog Science Fiction and Fact,' 'Artemis Magazine,' 'Mensa Bulletin,' and 'The SFWA Bulletin.' She lives in Florida with her husband, daughter, three cats, a dog, and seven chickens.

Richard Cartwright learned the fine art of storytelling sitting around kitchen tables, campfires and courtrooms over the years. He came to writing after getting out of the legal profession while he could still get his soul back. These days he manages a remote support team to feed his writing habit.

Speculative fiction author _Sophie G. Michaels_ loves the rich storytelling of the past and the possibilities of the future, bringing them both to life in her work. Her published works include 'Homecoming,' 'The Battle of Anderida Forest,' 'Return to Bethlehem,' *While Rivers Flow*, and *The Saga of Baldar and Brithwynn*.

Sarah Arnette writes fantasy and science fiction and is a reader of everything. She is a wife, mommy to two loving pitbulls, and has an imagination powerful enough to create galaxies of wonder. Surrounded by her books, it was only a matter of time before their whispers found their way into her mind, creating worlds that had to escape through her. A full listing of her books can be obtained at www.ArnetteBooks.com.

Stephanie Osborn, award-winning Interstellar Woman of Mystery, is a 20+-year space program veteran with multiple STEM degrees. She has authored, co-authored, or contributed to some 60 books, including *Burnout, Displaced Detective, Gentleman Aegis, EMPIRE, We Shall Rise*, and the *Division One & Blood Brothers* series, her take on the urban legend of mysterious people who make evidence...disappear. Find her books at www.Stephanie-Osborn.com.

Dale Kesterson (author, singer, actress, photographer, and hand-crafter) has lived everywhere from Long Island to a tiny Kansas town too small for a traffic light. She currently pens *The Lauren Kaye Mystery* series for Jumpmaster Press, and enjoys stepping outside her primary genre for special projects while living with her husband of over 50 years and their hairless cats.

Editor Biographies

Stephanie Osborn, award-winning Interstellar Woman of Mystery, is a 20+-year space program veteran, with graduate/undergraduate degrees in astronomy, physics, chemistry and mathematics, and is "fluent" in several more subjects. Author, co-author, or contributor to some 60 titles, including the celebrated _Burnout: The mystery of Space ShuttleSTS-281_, parts of the _Cresperian Saga_ and the _EMPIRE_ series, the _Displaced Detective_ series, the award-winning _Gentleman Aegis_ series, and the _Division One_ series and its spinoff _Blood Brothers_. She "pays it forward," teaching STEM through numerous media including ebooks, radio, podcasting and public speaking, and working with SIGMA, the science-fiction think tank. She also edits free-lance as well as for Chromosphere Press. Find her books, or contact her for editing, at www.Stephanie-Osborn.com.

Jon Nials is a software and site reliability engineer, who has worked at numerous startups and Fortune 500 companies. He has worked as a farmhand, and many other manual labor jobs, all of which motivated him to get a job with air conditioning. He studied chemistry until he blew up the lab three times. He is the widowman of the love of his life, has 4 biological children, and many other children who call him Dad. Coming from a line of farmers and teachers, he values hard work and learning. He reads ancient Greek and encyclopedia entries for fun.

www.ingramcontent.com/pod-product-compliance
Lightning Source LLC
Chambersburg PA
CBHW021336190726
48288CB00003B/1135